"I'd do anything for you."

Her chest tightened at his words as she wished for things that she'd written off. Things too painful to think about.

"Jade..." Ethan pulled in a ragged breath. She'd give anything to know what he was thinking, but here in the middle of the wilderness, with the threat of Div's army finding them, was not the place for this conversation.

He dropped his hand. "We'd better get across the bridge."

Jade's breathing was anything but steady as she followed. So far, there was no sign of anyone close.

She stepped onto the wooden bridge. "I don't like this." The words slipped out as they headed to the opposite side. Water rushed beneath them. She drew her weapon, and Ethan did the same. "Something feels off."

"Agreed. Let's hurry."

Halfway across the bridge, a noise behind them had her whirling. "What was that?"

Before Ethan could answer, the crack of a weapon split the tension.

Mary Alford was inspired to become a writer after reading romantic suspense greats Victoria Holt and Phyllis A. Whitney. Soon, creating characters and throwing them into dangerous situations that tested their faith came naturally for Mary. In 2012, Mary entered the speed dating contest hosted by Love Inspired Suspense and later received "the call." Writing for Love Inspired Suspense has been a dream come true for Mary.

Books by Mary Alford

Love Inspired Suspense

Forgotten Past
Rocky Mountain Pursuit
Deadly Memories
Framed for Murder
Standoff at Midnight Mountain
Grave Peril
Amish Country Kidnapping
Amish Country Murder
Covert Amish Christmas
Shielding the Amish Witness
Dangerous Amish Showdown
Snowbound Amish Survival
Amish Wilderness Survival
Amish Country Ransom

Visit the Author Profile page at LoveInspired.com.

AMISH COUNTRY RANSOM

MARY ALFORD

LOVE INSPIRED SUSPENSE

INSPIRATIONAL ROMANCE

LOVE INSPIRED® SUSPENSE
INSPIRATIONAL ROMANCE

Recycling programs for this product may not exist in your area.

ISBN-13: 978-1-335-59901-8

Amish Country Ransom

Love Inspired
22 Adelaide St. West, 41st Floor
Toronto, Ontario M5H 4E3, Canada
www.LoveInspired.com

Printed in U.S.A.

What time I am afraid, I will trust in thee.
—*Psalm* 56:3

For my husband. You are always my hero.

ONE

A shrilling phone filled his troubled dreams of Afghanistan...until Ethan Connors forced his eyes open. Soon the chaos of battle evaporated, and the living room of his house near the West Kootenai, Montana, Amish community replaced deadly scenes from the past.

His attention landed on the photo of his wife, Jolie—or Lee as she preferred to be called. It was her father's pet name for her because *Jolie* sounded too old-fashioned. Every time he looked at her picture on his fireplace mantel, he was reminded of how much he'd let her down in those final years before her death.

The phone continued to blast Ethan's favorite ringtone, and Molly, his German shepherd and constant companion, leapt to her feet as if sensing trouble. Molly was a former military dog who had seen plenty of dangerous situations during her multiple tours of duty. She knew when to be concerned, and she was now.

Several hours had passed since Ethan had slipped into his favorite chair intending to only rest for a minute. Now, it was late afternoon, and he'd been asleep for a while after a particularly grueling morning of training with the dogs.

As part of the county's search and rescue team, Ethan was used to getting calls at all hours of the day. You never knew when someone would go missing. But this call had him worried from the second he got a look at the number.

Jade Powell.

Jade wasn't much for casual conversation. If she was calling, then something was up. Instinctively, his hand tightened on the phone as he swiped to answer the call. "What's wrong?"

"Help me." The words were lower than a whisper—barely distinguishable as belonging to the strong woman Ethan knew Jade to be.

He sat up straighter. She'd been one of his—a former soldier who had served under his command...until Jade had been attacked, severely injured and had left the Marines. They'd been recently reunited quite by accident while she was working undercover for the FBI on a case in which Ethan and another former marine, Tanner Mast, had been kidnapped. Jade had been instrumental in saving Ethan's life.

"Jade?" He waited through several seconds of labored breathing on the other end. It sounded as if she were running. "Jade, are you still there?"

Ethan checked the phone to make sure the call was still connected. It was. "Tell me what's going on?" The only answer was more frantic breathing sounds.

And then…

"He's here." Those two forced words came through the phone with frightening clarity. "Ethan, he's here, and he has her." *He's here.* Ethan had no doubt whom Jade spoke of. The very thought of the monster who had viciously kidnapped and attacked her in Afghanistan being here in West Kootenai was unfathomable.

Ethan shot to his feet, which elicited a low growl from Molly.

"Where are you? I'll come get you." The silence that followed was terrifying. The ghost from Jade's past known only as "Div" had found her.

"Jade, are you still at your cabin?" Nothing but static. Then silence. Ethan glanced at his phone and realized the call was lost. By Jade's hand…or had something happened to her? He redialed without any response.

"Let's go, Molly." His fear for Jade's safety had him heading for the door. Ethan grabbed his jacket and shoved his feet into his boots while calling his friend and business partner, Fletcher Shetler.

Fletcher answered almost immediately.

"I need you and Mason to meet me at the Dennison cabin up Evergreen Road." Ethan and Fletcher had begun training search and rescue dogs several months back. The process was intense, but they had a promising group of animals, and he enjoyed working with the dogs immensely. Mason, Fletcher's brother, was one of Ethan's partners in a hunting guide business and also a member of the SAR team.

Ethan grabbed a backpack that held the equipment he used for the SAR missions. He stepped out into the freezing afternoon while doing his best to explain the call from Jade. Both brothers were acquainted with her.

"I'm almost positive this is the same person who hurt Jade in Afghanistan. From what I could gather before I lost the call, he has Jade's sister, Rose." During Jade's tour of duty years back, she'd learned of a dangerous weapons smuggler and tried to have him investigated. Ethan had reported what Jade had witnessed in the desert and heard from her asset, a young local woman named Arezo. But once Ethan made the report, it was as if all traces of the illegal organization had disappeared in the swirling sands of Afghanistan. A few days later, Arezo had been taken from her house at gunpoint by a masked assailant. She was never seen again. The military turned the case over to the local authorities, yet Jade hadn't been able to let it go.

A few nights later, Jade was kidnapped and brutally attacked while on patrol. She'd been warned to keep out of what didn't concern her. Jade had almost died, which seemed to prove that this smuggler—whoever he might be— wasn't about to let anyone stand in his way. Not even a US soldier.

Though Jade had given the authorities what few details she could remember, she hadn't seen Div's face and nothing had ever come of it. After the attack, Jade had changed. She'd become more withdrawn. Before being discharged, she'd spent the rest of her time in Afghanistan—even though she'd barely been able to walk because of the injuries she'd sustained during her kidnapping—trying to find the young woman or at least get some answers for her family. When they returned stateside and Ethan learned she'd joined the FBI, he had no doubt she would continue to work the case whenever possible using their resources. Had her inquiries somehow brought her attacker to her door?

"Do we know for certain she's at the cabin?" Fletcher asked.

Ethan didn't and told his friend as much. "I lost the call before Jade could tell me. We'll start at her cabin. Hopefully, there will be some clue as to what's really happening."

"I'll call Mason right away," Fletcher said. "We'll meet you there. If this is related to what happened in Afghanistan, every second she's missing and out there alone she's in danger. From this man who is coming after her *and* from the weather."

Fletcher's words ripped into Ethan's heart. Jade had been through enough. All he wanted to do was protect her.

"Thanks, Fletcher." Ethan ended the call with a small sense of relief that his friends would be at his side.

Fletcher and Mason were Amish, but because of their work with the SAR team, they were both allowed to carry cell phones, and the bishop had granted Mason permission to use a vehicle.

Ethan slung his backpack over his shoulder. A howling wind slapped him hard, and its biting chill seemed to bore right through him. Soon, snow covered his knit cap and jacket.

As he hunkered low against the cold, Ethan headed toward the training facility that housed his dogs while Molly trotted out in front of him.

Nimshi and Trackr, the two younger Saint

Bernards, must have heard them approaching over the wind and come out to investigate. He'd take them along with Molly.

"Are you two ready to go to work?" Both seemed to understand what he meant and barked enthusiastically.

Ethan headed inside, where Radar and Dakota, the two bloodhounds, bounded over to see what was happening along with Kit, the bluetick coonhound. All had plenty of pent-up energy despite their rigorous training earlier.

"Maybe next time, guys." He gave the remaining dogs some petting before grabbing the equipment needed to gear up the two Saint Bernards.

With both dogs' collars in place, he attached the leashes and started for the four-wheel-drive pickup with an enclosed bed parked in the garage close by. He loaded Nimshi and Trackr into the backseat and tossed his equipment bag inside the bed before getting Molly into the passenger seat.

As soon as he left the garage, his gaze swept the place that had been his home for so long, and as always, he thought about Lee. She'd wanted him to leave the military for years before he finally made the decision. When he'd returned stateside, he'd come home to the devastating news that his wife had cancer. She was dying.

Losing her had ripped out a chunk of his heart that would never return. Though his friends had told him it was time to move on—meet someone new—that part of his life was over. His entire purpose now had become focused on finding fulfillment in helping others. How could he let another woman down the way he had Lee?

As he hit the edge of his property, the phone rang. Mason Shetler's number appeared on the screen.

"Sorry to bring you out in this weather," he told his friend. Mason had a young family, and a mother-in-law who suffered from Huntington's disease. Not to mention how hard he worked farming his land.

"It's no problem. I couldn't sleep anyway. The wind is really screaming, isn't it? I'm afraid the storm is just getting started."

"I agree. Let's pray it isn't a bad one, and this all proves just a huge mistake. Hopefully, we'll find both Jade and Rose at their house safe and sound." Yet the pit in his stomach wouldn't let Ethan believe that for a second. He knew her backstory, and it was every bit as scary as the call he'd received from Jade earlier.

"I'm a few minutes out from picking up Fletcher. We'll meet you at the cabin."

"Thanks, brother." Ethan ended the call and tried Jade's number again. When there was no answer, he reached out to his friend, Sheriff Walker Collins, with the same result. The town of Eagle's Nest was on the other side of the mountain range, and the incoming weather was interrupting the cell signal. This was the last thing he needed when he could use the sheriff's help. Ethan shoved the phone back into his pocket.

He kept replaying the fear he'd heard in Jade's voice. She was tough as nails. Even after the attack in Afghanistan, she hadn't shown any cracks in her armor...except when anyone got too close.

Ethan glanced into the backseat where the dogs had settled down, waiting for their chance to track. They loved this work, and they were good at it. Molly had been responsible for helping to locate Ethan and Tanner when they'd been kidnapped and taken into the Kootenai National Forest. Ethan would put her tracking skills up against any of the younger dogs.

Snow and sleet had been falling for some time now. He clicked the wipers on and leaned forward to see more clearly. This early storm had hit the area unexpectedly. Though it was still fall, the weather this time of year could be unpredictable.

Ethan almost missed the turnoff to the cabin. He braked hard, sending the truck skidding on the slick road. The dogs all sat up in their seats, watching as he recovered and slowly turned onto the gravel road. Through the snow flitting across the glow of the headlights, he studied the road for any sign that there had been someone up it recently. Whatever tracks there might have been had long since been covered by several inches of snow.

On a couple of occasions, he'd visited Jade and her sister here at their cabin. Rose was the younger of the two Powell sisters, and at twenty-four she was studying to become a police officer.

After being kidnapped and almost dying a couple of months back, Ethan had felt a connection to Jade that was different from when she'd been under his command more than five years before. They'd both been through something life-threatening. He admired her courage. Jade had gone to great lengths to save him and Tanner from the clutches of a drug kingpin—and had put her own life in danger to do it. He owed her a lot.

Ethan eased the truck up the road until he reached the dark cabin. The first thing to grab him as troubling was the sight of Jade's Jeep parked in front of the house. The driver's door stood open—as if she'd left it in a hurry.

He has her...

Those simple words held the worst possible news. Div had taken Rose. Did he now have Jade as well?

"Stay. I'll be back," he told the two Saint Bernard dogs while letting Molly out. The German shepherd didn't waste time, sniffing first the air and then the ground for any viable scents.

Ethan grabbed his handgun and followed. He should wait until his backup arrived. After all, Mason had once been a US marshal. He knew how to handle himself in a dangerous situation. Yet the call from Jade wouldn't let him sit by and wait. She was in trouble. She needed him.

Though it was daylight, the weather made it hard to see clearly. Ethan clicked on his flashlight and whisked it around on the ground. Nothing of any use. Even Jade's footprints had been covered by the snow. He felt the hood of the Jeep. It was cold.

While snow normally made it easier for the dogs to detect smells, heavy snowfall—such as what was moving in quickly—could prevent the scent from dissipating into the air where the dogs could follow it. In freezing conditions such as these, the water in the air would freeze and suppress the scents. In other words, time was critical. He and the dogs needed to get on the trail as soon as possible.

The cabin was nestled at the end of the dead-end road. There was nothing beyond this point except wilderness and rugged mountain terrain.

Help me...

Jade needed him to figure out what had happened to her and Rose quickly.

His attention went to a single set of headlights approaching. Uneasiness tightened the muscles in his back. Ethan grabbed his phone and hit Mason's number again, thankful when the call went through. "Is that you I see coming?"

"It is. Any sign of Jade?"

"Not yet. I haven't searched the house." He explained about her Jeep being left out in the weather instead of parked in the detached garage. "She wouldn't have left it out in the elements without a good cause. I tried Walker's number. The weather is playing havoc with the signal, I guess. I couldn't reach him."

"That's not *gut*. I only see your tracks. If they've taken her, how did they get her out?" Mason asked the question on Ethan's mind as well.

"Maybe they didn't. Perhaps Jade escaped her attackers, and they're searching for her." Still, they'd need transportation up to the cabin, which meant there should be tracks. A shudder worked through him as he glanced up at the mountain rising through the trees. "I'll see you when you get here." Ethan punched End and stepped up on the porch.

This was bad in so many ways. He tried the door and wasn't surprised to find it unlocked. With his handgun in front of him, Ethan entered the house and clicked on the overhead light. There was no sign that a struggle had taken place inside. A fire had burned to embers in the fireplace. There were breakfast dishes in the sink. Whatever had happened to Jade and to Rose hadn't started here.

Headlights swept the front of the house. Seconds later, Mason and Fletcher came inside.

"Anything?" Fletcher said and glanced around the living space.

Ethan shook his head. "I haven't searched all of the place yet, but I don't believe Jade or her sister were taken from here."

"We'll check the rest of the house," Mason assured him. "Try Sheriff Collins again."

Ethan immediately retrieved his phone to call his good friend. He and the sheriff had become close following several dangerous incidents that had occurred in the community, with which Ethan had assisted.

After three tries without the call going through, Ethan reluctantly accepted the truth. The weather was preventing his call from connecting with the sheriff. He tried getting a text message out with the same results.

Mason and his brother returned to the living room.

"There's no sign of either woman," Fletcher confirmed.

Ethan ran his hand over his eyes. "I can't reach Walker either. Looks like we're going to have to do this on our own."

Mason's keen eyes found him. "And we don't fully understand what we're up against. If this is the guy you spoke about, he's clearly dangerous."

The words had Ethan's midsection tightening. If this was Jade's trouble in Afghanistan coming back to haunt her, how had Div found her here in such a remote location?

He recalled seeing the case that Jade had worked recently mentioned in the news. She'd been helping take down drug smuggler Zeke Bowman, but since Jade was undercover, the Bureau had been careful to keep her out of the publicity that followed. Had someone inadvertently leaked her association with the case?

"Let's get the dogs," Ethan said. "If Jade's Jeep is here, then we know she made it this far. Since she's not in the house, the only other place she could have gone is up the mountain." With the weather continuing to deteriorate, traversing the woods on the mountainside wasn't going to be easy. "I'll see if I can find something in her vehicle to help the dogs train on her scent."

Ethan grabbed his backpack from the truck and then headed to Jade's Jeep, where he found a dark green knit cap. He grabbed it and let each of the dogs pick up the scent. In a matter of seconds, the three were searching. Molly picked up the trail and dashed into the woods north of the house. They were heading straight for the high country where the weather would be far worse, making the unknown danger facing them that much deadlier.

Each breath felt like knives stabbing her chest. Jade Powell had barely managed to fight off the mercenaries who'd been lying in wait for her when she entered the woods. Being forced into hand-to-hand combat was something she should have expected, should have foreseen. Until she'd heard his voice, she hadn't wanted to believe it, but now there was no doubt. The weapons smuggler from her past was here in Montana, and he had her sister, Rose.

She'd been jumped before she'd reached the spot where she was supposed to meet Div. Under normal circumstances, Jade knew better than to go into a dangerous situation without backup, but Div had threatened to kill Rose if he saw any hint of another person besides her. She didn't have a choice. She'd walked straight into an ambush.

Somehow, she'd managed to escape after being badly beaten. That was over an hour ago. So far, Jade had eluded her attackers, but she knew they were out there looking for her.

The call to Ethan had dropped before she could give critical details about her location. He was the closest possible option for help, and she knew Ethan would search until he found her. The terror she'd felt at hearing Div's voice when he'd called her earlier brought back everything from the attack that night in Afghanistan. She'd lived in a state of perpetual fear ever since, suspended in that moment in time when everything changed. Unable to move forward, make connections, let anyone close to her. Having a normal relationship was impossible. Because of what happened, she'd ended her romance with her high-school sweetheart, Stephen, and until recently her relationship with Rose had been strained.

After the terrible things Jade had endured at Div's hands, she'd retreated into herself and hadn't been there for Rose when her sister had needed her. Fixing their relationship had taken a lot of hard work, and it was still a work in progress.

When she'd called Rose earlier today to check in, her sister hadn't answered. Then on her way home from the FBI office in Missoula, she'd gotten a call from Rose's number…only it wasn't her sister but the voice of the man she'd never forget. That call had as good as confirmed his identity to Jade. This was Div.

He'd laughed at her crippling silence—had known exactly how terrified she was of him. She'd tried to get him to tell her his name, but he told her he liked the name she and Arezo used. Jade's heart had plummeted. In Middle Eastern folklore, the name Div meant *monster*, and that was exactly what he was in Jade's mind.

When she'd heard Div speak, it had reinforced the truth in her mind. He was an American. She'd detected a Midwestern accent when he'd taunted her years ago following the beating she'd taken at his hands in Afghanistan.

Why had an American been smuggling guns in Afghanistan, and how had Div ended up here in Montana? There was no way this was a coincidence.

Div had told her to meet him at a specific location up the wooded mountainside and to come alone, without FBI backup, if she wanted to see her sister alive again. He insisted she bring the evidence she'd gathered on him. He'd exchange it for Rose. How had he known she'd been following him?

Jade had thought she'd been so careful when she and Rose had noticed suspicious activity in the area and had kept tabs on it. Jade hadn't taken it to the FBI because she told herself she needed further proof it was Div. But the truth was, after what he'd put her through, Jade wanted to be the one to bring him down. Wanted him to see her face when she did it.

Now Div had Rose, and Jade was terrified she'd lose her sister. She'd stashed the thumb drive holding their surveillance photos in a secret compartment in the Jeep, cautiously entered the wilderness and walked straight into an ambush.

She ducked behind a tree now to catch her breath and scoured the woods behind her. No sign of them. Bending over, her hands on her knees, she pulled in a handful of breaths that sent pain radiating from her bruised ribs to her swollen face. She had to keep moving. She gathered a few more breaths and started running again, her frantic thoughts replaying the brief conversation she'd had with the man who still had the power to haunt her nightmares.

She'd been foolish letting Rose come with her on the fact-finding expedition in the first place. Her sister wanted to help because she knew how personal this was to Jade, and Rose desired to be a police officer someday. She'd be starting her training soon and thought the stakeout could be useful. But Rose wasn't ready to face this kind of danger. And now *he* had her.

The tiniest of sounds grabbed her away from those thoughts. Once more, she took cover and peeked out. Nothing visible. Maybe it was an animal roaming the woods? The knot in her gut wouldn't let her believe it.

Jade shoved away from the tree and ran. She had no idea where this direction would lead, and she couldn't keep up this pace forever. Already, she could feel herself slowing down.

If only she could rewrite the events of the day. She would have insisted Rose go with her to Missoula to the FBI field office. Jade's supervisor had wanted to discuss the upcoming court case against the drug smuggler Zeke Bowman in person.

When Jade had asked Rose to come along, her sister told her she was tired and planned to stay home and catch up on some rest. Jade should have known it wasn't the truth.

She now believed Rose had returned to the place near the Canadian border that she and Jade had been watching for days as massive amounts of something were being moved into the US.

Swiping a hand across her forehead, Jade glanced over her shoulder, unable to shake the feeling that her attackers were closing in. They would keep coming because the alternative of letting her go free would probably mean their own deaths.

She stared at the endless woods in front of her and tried to make the right decision.

Lord, I sure could use Your help...

She and Rose had grown up believing in God. They'd attended church devotedly with their parents. But she'd lost sight of her faith for a long time until what happened in Afghanistan. Jade would never have survived any of it without God's protective hand on her.

It took far longer than it should have to realize the tiniest of out-of-place sounds interrupting her prayer were her worst fear coming to fruition. Footsteps.

She ran harder. After covering only a handful of feet, the world around her exploded. Gunshots lit up the woods. *Keep going!* The frantic thought raced through her head.

Jade blindly returned fire, hopefully forcing her hunters to take cover while she pressed on as fast as her injured body would allow. She couldn't get caught. Rose's life was on the line.

Her brief reprieve didn't last long before another all-out assault on her life started up again.

She screamed as one of the bullets pierced through her side. She'd been hit.

Jade struggled to keep going. *Put one foot in front of the other.* The shooting continued though the sound of it blurred along with the world around her. She was in real trouble.

Somehow, Jade managed to retrieve her phone from where she'd stashed it in her jacket pocket. She quickly tried to call Ethan without success. No one knew she was out here. The thought was terrifying.

She slumped against a tree and slid down to the ground, helpless to stop herself. The weapon shook in her hand. Footsteps—they were almost right on top of her. She pulled in a ragged breath and struggled to stay focused, to aim the weapon, but she couldn't.

Someone came closer.

"No." She did her best to hold the weapon steady enough to fire. Images of what Div had done to her in Afghanistan poured through her head. She couldn't go through that again.

"Jade." She recognized the voice immediately, and the relief it brought was weakening.

"Ethan?" The weapon slipped from her hand. If she were capable of showing physical expression, she would have hugged him. Ethan had found her. When she'd made the call to him, Jade had known he would move heaven and earth to get to her. That was why she'd called him—beyond the fact that he was closer than her FBI colleagues. Ethan had the heart of a protector, and he'd been protecting her since the attack in Afghanistan. He was still every bit as strong and physically fit as he had been when he'd led their unit, and he would fight to the death to save her.

Ethan lowered his six-foot-plus frame down beside her. Snow clung to his heavy camo jacket. His jeans and boots were soaked from the snowfall. He wore a black knit cap pulled down over his chestnut brown hair, which was cut short in military fashion—the only way she'd ever seen it. The concern in his blue eyes was all for her. That same nervous feeling she'd experienced recently whenever he came to visit her was there to remind Jade that as damaged as she was, she was not immune to being attracted to her handsome former lieutenant.

There were two Amish men with him. She recognized Fletcher and Mason Shetler. They'd become friends in recent weeks, and she admired the Amish way of life greatly. There were many times when Jade found herself wishing she could go back in time to a simpler period for herself and Rose.

"How'd you find me?" She barely recognized her own voice. It sounded so raspy.

"The dogs." Ethan spotted a dark stain on her red jacket and frowned. "How bad is it?" Those intense blue eyes held hers while she tried to think beyond the fog of injury.

"Just a graze." But it hurt intensely, and she was losing blood.

"We need to get her out of the weather to examine the wound," Ethan said to Mason.

"There's an old, abandoned cabin up ahead. I think the shooters have scattered, but we can't afford to stay there long."

"Understood." Ethan rose. "Can you stand?" he asked Jade.

She nodded even though she wasn't nearly so certain. Jade stumbled to her feet with the help of Ethan's hand and slumped against him.

He put his arm around her shoulder. "I've got you." Those whispered words had never been so welcome before. She couldn't remember the last time someone had her. Probably when she was just a child. She always felt safe with Ethan. Until…

Normally, when anyone touched her, the old panic from the past would rise up inside and she would push them away. But Ethan was one of the few she trusted. And she needed his help.

With his assistance, they started moving, each of her breaths more labored than the one before. She stumbled several times and was actually grateful for Ethan's firm grip, otherwise she would have fallen.

Jade spotted three of Ethan's dogs and smiled. They'd saved her life. The dogs were a huge part of his life, and she'd gotten acquainted with the animals over the past few months since she and Ethan had reconnected. She'd even assisted in some of his training.

A dark silhouette appeared before them.

"There's the house," Fletcher said. He and Mason went on ahead.

Her injury forced Jade and Ethan to move at a slower pace. Each step drained her depleted energy at a frightening rate.

They finally reached the front entrance. "Are you going to be okay here by yourself?" he asked. "We need to clear the house before you go inside."

She forced herself to stand on her own while sweat beads formed on her forehead, mocking the effort. "I'm fine. Go."

With the two Amish following, Ethan stepped inside and immediately she was on edge. Jade leaned against the side of the house, her eyes darting around the woods. What had happened to the shooters? If they found her and the others, she, Ethan and the brothers would be trapped, but Ethan was right. She wouldn't be able to go far without the injury being treated.

"It's clear."

Jade jerked toward the sound of Ethan's voice. She realized she no longer had her weapon.

"Here." Ethan handed the Glock back to her. "You dropped it. Let's get you in and have a look at your side."

Jade followed him through the door. Her legs deserted her, and she collapsed against the rotted wooden floor.

"Rose. He has my sister." Her gaze found Ethan's. "We have to get her back. He'll kill her eventually. He's using her as leverage to get me to give him the information I've gathered on his operation here."

Time was running out for her sister. How long before Div realized that Rose would prove more of a liability than an asset? When that happened, her sister would be dead.

TWO

Ethan knelt beside Jade, his hands unsteady. Many people wanted her dead, and they wouldn't stop simply because of a little return fire. He'd need to get Jade bandaged up as quickly as possible so they could keep moving. Staying in one place was dangerous.

"Let me have a look at the wound." He gently pushed her jacket up. Jade shrank away. Ethan looked into green eyes filled with a terror he didn't understand. "Did I hurt you?"

Jade slowly shook her head, sending her dark hair swishing behind her. "No, it's just… I'm fine. Please, continue." She bit her bottom lip and looked so vulnerable.

Ethan remembered how frightened she'd been when she was found after being kidnapped and beaten in Afghanistan. Her body had been broken and bruised, yet she didn't want anyone to touch her then as well. He'd often wondered if Div had taken his punishment to a much more personal level and Jade had been raped, though she never mentioned it.

Was she having flashbacks of that time?

Her green plaid flannel shirt was covered in blood, and her jeans were spattered with it as well. Once he lifted her shirt up enough to see the injury, he blew out a relieved breath. "It's just a flesh wound." *Thank You, God.*

He removed his backpack and found gauze and bandages.

"What happened?" Ethan asked while he worked. "Your call seemed to indicate this is connected to the weapons smuggler from Afghanistan." He glanced up at her strained expression.

"There's no doubt in my mind that it is. He's here in Montana," she said without hesitation. "I found him. This is Div's work, Ethan. I can't explain how, but somehow, he's here."

Mason moved to the window with his brother to watch their surroundings.

"What do you mean *you* found him? How?" He finished cleaning the wound and then bandaged it.

"On the last case I worked, where you were kidnapped, I overheard Zeke Bowman mention he had a contact in Afghanistan who could get him weapons. I never thought in my wildest dreams it would be the same man." She explained about the meet Bowman had scheduled. Bowman never used a name, but it was clear he was a little afraid of the man he was meeting.

"It was him, Ethan. It was Div—I'm sure of it now." She waited for him to say something. When he didn't, she said, "Rose and I found where we believed he was bringing the weapons into the country but then I was called to Missoula." She stopped for a second before looking him in the eyes. "I think Rose went back there today. That's how he was able to take her. I didn't have a chance to check, but I'm sure her truck was missing from the garage."

Ethan nodded. She was right. There wasn't a truck parked in the garage.

Mason suddenly turned from the window, drawing their attention. "We've got company. I count at least three in the woods."

Before Ethan could reach the window, a slew of bullets flew into the house shattering the windows next to where the brothers had been standing. Mason and Fletcher hit the ground seconds before. Ethan and Jade ducked while shots continued to pepper the front of the house.

"We can't get away. We'll have to stand and fight," Jade whispered.

Ethan listened to the sounds of battle all around. A brief silence was quickly followed by more shooting. He crawled to the window and peered cautiously over the windowsill. He became aware of Jade on the opposite side. Gunshots illuminated the area where the shots came from, and Ethan aimed and fired. A scream followed shortly after. He'd struck one but had no idea how badly the shooter was injured.

Jade fired and hit a second target. The third man realized what was happening and ducked behind a tree before firing.

"Do you see him?" Jade asked as she continued searching for the gunman.

"Not yet, but hang on a second…" The man inched from behind his cover to fire. It was all Ethan needed. He shot once, and the perp dropped to the ground.

In the silence that followed, Ethan prayed there weren't more out there waiting for them to leave the protection of the house.

"We have to get out of here before anyone else shows up," Mason told them.

He was right. Ethan rose and started for the door after the brothers. Jade stood near the window without moving. "What's wrong? Are you hurt?" On her face, he saw her worst fears and soul-wrenching sadness all rolled up into one frightening expression.

She shook her head. "No, I'm okay. We can't just leave. He has Rose. I can't imagine what he'll do to her…no, actually, I can because I've been through it before, and I don't want my sister to experience what he put me through. Certainly not what he did to Arezo."

Having been abducted himself, he understood the fear going through Jade's mind right now. "We have no idea where he might have taken Rose. We need help, Jade," he said gently.

"I won't leave here without her." She squared her shoulders and stood her ground. "I borrowed Rose's jacket this morning before I left for Missoula because it's heavier and I knew it was going to get colder as the day progressed. I didn't think Rose would need it because she was supposed to stay home." She shook her head. "The dogs can track her from her scent on it, right?" He understood how hard this was for her, and how close she was to Rose, but still.

"Yes, but where do we even begin?" There was a lot of wilderness around and neither of them had any idea where Div had taken Rose.

"I overheard one shooter saying *he* wanted me brought to him alive." Ethan stared at her, trying to understand the meaning of her words. "Ethan, I think he took Rose to the same place we saw the weapons—or what we believed to be weapons—being moved into the country."

He ran his hand across his neck. The chances of the weapons smuggler staying in one place that long was slim if what had happened in Afghanistan was any indication. He'd disappeared like smoke upon being found out.

"We have to try, Ethan," she insisted, her pleading eyes holding his.

He'd do whatever he could to help Jade find her sister. Ethan cared about her, had done his best to protect her in Afghanistan and failed. He wouldn't fail again.

Fletcher glanced between them. "What are we doing, folks? Because every bad guy in the area has heard those shots by now."

"We're not going to give up," Ethan told her. "But Fletcher's right—our assailants will have called for backup by now. There may even be others in the woods now searching for you. We don't really know what we're up against. We need help."

"There's no time, and the phones aren't working because of the weather. Please—she's all I have." She stepped closer, her emerald green eyes holding him hostage.

She pushed raven hair from her eyes. He'd always marveled at how deceptively fragile Jade appeared even though she was almost as tall as he was.

She was trained in several forms of martial arts. She could defeat any man she went up against. He believed her need to be the best in all forms of hand-to-hand combat was a result of what had happened in the desert. She wanted to protect herself.

"All right." He gave in with a heavy sigh while wondering if this would be another mistake that might cost lives. "We'll keep going."

Mason went outside with Fletcher.

Jade's face broke into a smile. She quickly removed the jacket she was wearing and held it out to Molly first, and then Nimshi and Trackr. The dogs immediately picked up the scent and charged from the house while Jade swung toward him once more. "She's been in this area at one time," she said in a stunned voice.

"You're right." He stepped out into the weather and got his bearings. Jade stopped beside him, her coat back on. He could almost feel the turmoil going on inside her. Though the man who had taken Arezo had worn a disguise, and there was no way to prove he was Div, Jade seemed certain it was him and just as positive that he'd killed Arezo, even though her body was never found. If this was Div's work and he had Rose, he couldn't imagine how frightened Jade must be.

"We'll find her." Ethan shifted her way. The woman standing beside him had been through so much in her life, and yet she was still standing strong.

"Thank you, Ethan," she said sincerely. "I don't know what I'd do without you."

He skimmed her pretty face, and something he hadn't felt in a long time tightened his chest. He couldn't deny that she was a beautiful woman, and he'd found himself thinking of her like that many times lately, but Lee had been his everything. At times, he still couldn't believe she was gone. Being attracted to Jade felt like ripping a bandage off a wound. It hurt too much, and he felt as if he were betraying the love of his life.

Ethan cleared his throat. With a final glance he added, "We'd better keep going."

Once he'd reached the location of the first shooter, Ethan checked for a pulse and didn't find one. A quick search of pockets confirmed the man had no identification on him, probably deliberately. That would make it harder to link him to Div.

"Ethan, take a look at this?" Jade called him over to where she stood near another deceased.

Ethan grabbed the dead man's weapon and the extra magazine in his jacket pocket before heading her way.

"This guy is carrying an M4 rifle. And I found an M24 sniper rifle on that man over there." Jade's gaze locked with his. "This is

Div's MO. Arezo reported that he and his goons were stealing weapons from battle sites."

Stealing weapons was one thing, but the very fact that Div was here in the US hinted at something much larger in the works. Was it possible he had joined forces with someone with a whole lot of power?

Ethan kept that disturbing thought to himself.

"We should gather the weapons and keep moving," Mason told them. "The dogs appear to be on Rose's scent." Catching up with Molly and the others wasn't easy. Nimshi and Trackr were eager to prove themselves under Molly's leadership.

Fletcher scanned the woods around them as if expecting trouble.

While they hustled to keep with the dogs, Ethan stayed close to Jade. Though her gunshot wound wasn't life-threatening, it served as a reminder of what Div was capable of doing.

"How are you holding up?" He noticed her holding her injured side.

"I'm okay." She turned her head toward him. Her face was swollen where she'd been struck, and an ugly red mark ran across her cheek. Anger rose inside of him at such senseless evil. He'd witnessed it throughout his career in the military and even in this peaceful part of Montana.

"I promise it looks worse than it is. I'm really sorry I had to call you in, but there wasn't anyone else." Her hands clenched and unclenched at her side. She was hurt and afraid for her sister, but past anger was there as well. She wanted justice for Arezo and for herself for what Div had done.

Would her need for justice end up getting herself or someone else hurt?

He hated what she'd been forced to endure in Afghanistan and couldn't imagine how hard it was knowing the one responsible was still out there.

Jade swallowed as if fighting back emotions. She was one of the best marines he'd had the privilege to serve with. She'd always been able to compartmentalize her feelings when in battle. The only time he'd ever seen her show what was in her heart was when her informant had disappeared. Jade had blamed herself for what had happened to Arezo.

"Hey, you saved my life. The least I can do is return the favor," he said to lighten the moment.

She laughed, then winced and grabbed her side once more.

Up ahead, Mason stopped suddenly.

"What have you got?" Ethan asked when he and Jade caught up with the brothers.

Mason pointed to the broken plant life. The

multiple footprints in the snow. "Someone has been through here recently."

"Over here." Fletcher waved everyone to where something red dotted the snow. Blood.

"We don't know that it's Rose's." Ethan did his best to assure Jade. "It might belong to an animal, or perhaps one of our assailants escaped." Once more, he tried calling Walker with the same results. "This weather's not helping." He looked up at the gray skies.

Right now, he had no idea what was happening, but he had a feeling it went much deeper than smuggling some military weapons into the country. To understand, he needed to know everything Jade could tell him. "I need you to fill me in on what you and Rose witnessed near the border."

Jade shook her head. "If I hadn't been undercover in Bowman's organization, we might not have known about Div being in the US. I guess something good came from what happened." She glanced his way. "After I realized he might be in Montana, I went back to the ranch where Bowman met with him. Rose agreed to help me with the investigation because she knew it was personal for me. She and I sat on the place for days before there was any activity. It was a single SUV that left the ranch. We followed it to an isolated mountainous region several miles from the border. There were a few abandoned buildings at the site and an old house. We waited for several hours before we spotted at least five vehicles heading toward the place. Rose and I crept down as close as we could. We overheard several conversations in Dari." She waited for him to speak, but words wouldn't come.

The mention of one of the spoken languages of Afghanistan was too much of a coincidence for him to dismiss. What did a weapons smuggler have planned here on US soil?

THREE

"Did you understand what they were saying?" Ethan asked. She stared up at him blankly.

Over the past few months, he and Jade had gotten closer. He liked to think he'd seen a glimmer of the woman she'd once been before the attack in Afghanistan, but there were times, like now, when he could almost feel her retreating inside herself.

"Jade?" Ethan repeated and touched her arm. She flinched. He quickly removed his hand, while disgust rose inside him. Just another ugly gift from Div, and one Jade hadn't been able to overcome even after so many years had passed.

"Sorry," she murmured without looking at him. She rubbed her forehead. "I didn't catch all of what was said. My skills have gotten rusty since leaving the military. But I did hear one man mention something happening in two weeks."

"Did he say what?"

She shook her head. "No, but he indicated it was important to get everything in place beforehand, which sent up all sorts of warnings." She hesitated briefly before adding, "I think Div is working with someone, Ethan. Bowman's in custody, his organization in shambles. It can't be Bowman, but I believe it is someone with a lot of power. Enough to get those weapons across the border."

Criminal elements always had a way of connecting to those who could be beneficial, like Bowman had connected with Div.

"When Rose accidently tripped and made a sound, I was certain they heard us," she continued. "We made it back to our vehicle, but I'm not completely sure we weren't spotted, possibly even followed."

In Ethan's opinion, Div had probably been tracking Jade all along. Would he have expected Jade to find out about his operation in the US? Jade had been trying to locate Div all these years and he'd known it. He probably wasn't worried about her going to the FBI because he knew she wanted to bring him down. Why else would Jade not report what she'd witnessed to her superiors? Div had used Jade's need for revenge to make her vulnerable. By grabbing

Rose, Div had ensured Jade would do whatever was necessary to get her sister back.

On the path ahead, Molly remained the lead dog.

"I'm so worried about Rose. After what happened to Arezo…" Jade broke off and turned her head away while running a hand over her eyes.

"Hey…you can't give up. We'll get her back."

"I hope so," she murmured in a voice barely audible. "I can't lose my sister."

They'd help find her. Both Fletcher and Mason continually studied the ground as they walked. Both were skilled trackers. Ethan couldn't ask for anyone better to assist.

The Amish community of West Kootenai was widespread, and some of the houses were intermingled with many of the *Englischer* ranches near Ethan's place. Mason and his young family lived close by.

As they continued fighting their way through the snowy woods with the three dogs on point, Ethan tried to recall his limited knowledge of the lay of the land this high up. There were a few houses scattered up on this side of the mountain. Several had been abandoned like the one they'd found earlier. The harsh Montana winters, especially at this high altitude, made it difficult to live. There were a couple of Amish families who had settled up here and had adapted to the harsh environment.

While they might be able to take refuge should the weather grow worse, they'd be bringing their trouble to those peaceful families. Still, they'd need help once they found where Rose was being held because there was no way they could take on an international weapon smuggling ring on their own.

"Ethan!" The alarm in Jade's voice pierced his chaotic thoughts. A second later, his worst nightmare materialized. A gunshot. Someone was shooting at them again.

Ethan ran for the nearest tree coverage along with Jade and the dogs.

He glanced past her to the lodgepole pine trees near where Fletcher and Mason were hiding.

"Any idea which direction it came from?"

Fletcher nodded toward the direction they'd come. "Straight behind. That didn't sound like a shotgun blast. I'm guessing it's the one who got away. He must be tracking us."

Until they could neutralize the threat, they were stuck. "We can't go on with him shooting at us," Jade whispered. "He may have already called others to this location."

"I'll see if I can draw him out. Cover me," Ethan told her.

Jade nodded and checked her weapon's clip. "I'm almost empty, but I have the rifle I took earlier."

Ethan indicated what he had planned to his friends. Both nodded. Even though the Amish were pacifists, both Fletcher and Mason had come face-to-face with their share of dangerous situations.

Jade peered around the tree. "I don't see him," she whispered. "Be careful."

Ethan sucked in a breath and ran for the next set of trees ahead.

As soon as he was out in the open, the shooter opened fire. Ethan dove for cover as a shot whizzed by his head. Jade quickly engaged.

The shooter was holding his position somewhere off to Ethan's left.

Ethan glanced at Jade. She pointed to the sniper's location.

While Ethan prepared to make his next attempt, Jade fired again. Ethan covered his head. A loud scream was followed by a thud. Ethan quickly jumped to his feet and whirled toward the noise. The soldier had been only a few feet from Ethan's position.

"Are you *oke, bruder*?" Mason asked.

Though shaken, Ethan confirmed he was.

Jade checked for a pulse on the gunman and shook her head. "He's dead. I was hoping we could capture him alive to get information on where they might have taken Rose, but he was going to kill you." Jade searched his pockets. "He has a cell phone and some extra clips for his handgun."

"How many more are out here?" Fletcher asked, scanning the snowy woods.

"I don't know, but we need help." Ethan glanced down at the dead shooter. "Fletcher, you and Mason head down the mountain until you can find a spot where you can get ahold of Walker. Have him bring his deputies up here stat."

Mason shook his head. "It's too dangerous for you and Jade to remain here alone. Come with us. We can wait for the sheriff and his law officers before continuing."

"The dogs are still on track," Ethan told him. "I don't want to pull them off a hot trail. Jade and I will continue on." But if he and Jade ran into more armed enemies, they couldn't fight them all off.

"I'll go," Mason volunteered. "Fletcher can stay here with you."

Ethan shook his head. "It's too dangerous alone. Take Fletcher for protection. Jade and I will be okay on our own. Right now, it's critical we get help up here and fast."

Mason's opinion of this was easy to read.

"Go, we'll be fine," Ethan assured his friend. "I'll activate the radio transmission in all the dogs' collars. You should be able to track us."

But if the weather continued to deteriorate, that signal would be interrupted as well.

"Oke," Mason eventually agreed. "As soon as we have service we'll reach out to the sheriff, but then we're coming back to help."

Ethan smiled at his friend's determination. "Thank you."

Mason was used to dealing with dangerous fugitives and knew that when their backs were against the wall, they'd do whatever was necessary to avoid prison.

And Div had gotten good at avoiding getting caught. Ethan shared Jade's opinion that he wasn't acting alone. Was it possible someone in authority had been assisting the arms smuggler through the years? The thought was unnerving.

"Be careful," Ethan told the brothers. Both nodded before starting down the path. "Rose is strong," Ethan assured Jade, reading all the fears on her expressive face. "She'll be okay."

"I should never have allowed Rose to get involved in this. I know she's grown and wants to join the police force someday, but she's not ready for what this monster is capable of." She ran her hand through her tangled hair before tucking it into her jacket.

"Here." He dug out the knit cap he'd used to find Jade and handed it to her. "It will help keep you warm. The dogs are on Rose's scent. Let's press on."

Jade slowly nodded and focused on the three dogs, who were diligently focused on their trail.

"How far is this ranch where Bowman met up with Div from the border location?" Ethan asked, and she shifted her attention to him.

"Not far. A couple of miles maybe."

"You think you can find it again on foot if necessary?"

She didn't hesitate. "I can. I'll never forget it. The ranch is fairly large and roughly seven miles from the Canadian border. It's strange because it's in the middle of several other Amish ranches."

"You're kidding." Ethan knew there were Amish families scattered all around the Montana countryside, but that still seemed strange to him.

She nodded. "While at the ranch with Bowman, I could walk around even though the place was heavily guarded. I managed to slip away from the rest of Bowman's team undetected. That's when I overheard Bowman and this weapons smuggler talking. He was clearly angry with Bowman, and his voice was raised." She shuddered. "It was Div."

"But you weren't able to see him?"

She shook her head. "No. I'd been close when one of the guards spotted me and forced me to return to the vehicle."

Ethan couldn't understand why Div had come to the US. It couldn't just be to keep an eye on Jade. "Why is he here? I'm sure there are plenty of far more lucrative places to sell those stolen weapons that would be less risky to enter."

"I wondered the same thing. There has to be a reason why he would choose to bring his organization to the US. After seeing the amount of weaponry I believe he's moving into the country, I'm positive Div has graduated to something far more deadly than simply stealing weapons."

As the dogs kept a quick steady pace, Ethan's concern for Jade grew. She appeared to be struggling to keep up. She'd taken a beating—she'd been shot. Her whole body was hurt, especially her face, which had taken the brunt of the blows.

He'd need to take a look at her bandage again soon. They couldn't risk it getting infected.

Jade's sudden stop captured his attention. "What is it?" he asked.

A second later, he heard the same thing. Someone else was here.

With Ethan at her side, Jade ran for cover. Hearing anything over her staccato heartbeat was difficult. Where were the men tracking them?

Several tense seconds ticked by while Jade expected Div's people to close in on them, but that didn't happen.

A shot ricocheted through the woods nearby. Jade jumped in reaction. Ethan placed his arm around her shoulder and brought her closer. An instinctive gesture that he didn't think twice about. Yet for her, not wanting to pull away was a huge victory.

Her feelings for Ethan had been gradually shifting for some time now. Until Ethan came back into her life, Jade had thought she'd accepted the truth that she would never have a normal life. But Ethan reminded her she wasn't ready to write love out of her life.

Yet how could she give her heart to anyone when every time she closed her eyes, she saw the shadowy figure of Div, only to be replaced by Arezo's mother begging Jade to find her daughter? No matter what, when Div was brought to justice, she'd fly to Afghanistan and personally deliver the news of his arrest.

She and Ethan had a lot in common.

Ethan had suffered a lot in his personal life as well. Losing his wife had been a particularly dark time for him. She understood the debilitating effects of grief. She'd felt it herself when her father had been convicted of setting those fires, which had resulted in two deaths. Jade hadn't thought she'd come back from the loss of losing him first to prison and then later to death.

She edged around the tree enough to see. An Amish guy carrying a shotgun was a welcome sight. "It's okay," she told Ethan. "He's Amish."

As soon as they stepped from their protection, the Amish man froze, his attention on their weapons.

"We mean you no harm," Ethan assured him before tucking his weapon into his jacket. Jade did the same.

"Why are you here?" he asked with suspicion. "In this weather." He clearly wasn't convinced they didn't intend on harming him.

Not that Jade could blame him. They'd appeared out of nowhere and were both armed.

"We're looking for someone. A young woman who has been taken against her will." Ethan explained that he was with the SAR team. "Have you seen anyone unusual around the area?"

The Amish gentleman shifted the shotgun to the opposite shoulder. "There was plenty of shooting earlier."

Jade's heart sank. That had been theirs. "Are there any other houses up this way?"

He confirmed with a nod. "There are several other Amish homes. One on the other side of the range. We all try to look after each other."

"Thank you for your time. All the best with

your hunting," Ethan told him before he and Jade started after the dogs once more.

"Wait, there was something strange that happened earlier in the day…"

Jade looked to Ethan before they turned back to the Amish man.

"What was it?" Jade prompted when the man hesitated, almost as if he still didn't trust them.

"I was doing chores when I noticed several vehicles moving along the road that we use to connect our places. They looked to be military-type vehicles."

Jade shot Ethan a look. "How many were there?"

He stroked his beard as he considered the question. "Probably half a dozen."

"When was this again?" Ethan asked.

"Several hours ago."

"Hang on a second." Jade remembered she had a recent photo on her phone of Rose. She brought it up. "Do you know if this woman was part of the group?" She showed him the photo.

He shook his head. "I can't say. I only saw the driver of the first vehicle. They were heading past my neighbors. I spoke to Elam after they'd left the area. He said the vehicles went past his house. Elam followed and watched their progress for a bit. He said the vehicles were heading east."

The idea that military vehicles were up here was disturbing. There weren't any military bases close by. So, who did these vehicles belong to?

Jade couldn't get Div's possible involvement out of her head. "Thank you for your help." Ethan shook the Amish man's hand before nodding to Jade.

Once the Amish gentleman was out of earshot, Jade tried to make sense of where those vehicles might be heading. "From here, east will take us close to the border and the place where we spotted the SUVs, but this is the first I've heard of military vehicles being used by Div. During my surveillance with Rose, they were using SUVs. I have no idea how the military vehicles fit into what's happening at the border."

Ethan's frown deepened. "I have no idea either, but whatever it is, it can't be good."

FOUR

Ethan couldn't get the Amish man's words out of his head. Where had so many military vehicles come from and how were they related to the suspected weapons smuggling across the border? How did Div get the weapons across in the first place? He shared his concerns with Jade.

"There's only one explanation. Someone at the border patrol has been paid to allow the crossing." Jade tugged her jacket tighter around her frame and winced when she touched her injured side. "But why now—after so long? Where's he been for so long?"

And, more importantly in Ethan's mind, why had he chosen to move his operation into the US? What was his endgame?

It had been years since the incident in Afghanistan. Ethan had kept in touch with his former military buddies, many of whom were now high up in the chain of command or had moved into intelligence. Though it was impossible to know every single threat that was coming their way, the intelligence community was actively pursuing all possible leads, especially those involving weapons smuggling.

Ethan had made a point of keeping Div's crimes in front of his intelligence friends. There had been no word of him since the incident in Afghanistan.

"What have you found out about Div through the years?" he asked Jade because he had no doubt she'd been searching for the gun smuggler.

She hesitated for a long beat.

"Jade?" he pressed when she remained quiet.

She sighed deeply. "Nothing really, but there was something unusual that happened. While I can't confirm it is him, I'm positive someone has been keeping track of me ever since I returned stateside."

The news was as alarming as it was surprising. "You're kidding? Why do you think someone has been following you?" And more importantly, why hadn't she told him about this before? They'd talked a lot recently. It hurt that she hadn't trusted him with this secret.

"I didn't want to worry you, Ethan," she answered his unasked question. "Especially after your wife died..." Her voice trailed off. Jade hadn't been at the funeral, but she'd sent him a heartfelt letter postmarked from Alaska.

The need to protect her grew as he looked into her beautiful face. Jade was important to him. She'd become a good friend. Still, every time he looked at her, he wished things could be different. Wished he could give her the impossible—what the guilt in his heart wouldn't allow him to give.

She looked his way. "You have to understand, I was so messed up when I got home. I didn't fit in anywhere. Rose needed me, but I couldn't be there for her either." She shook her head.

He recalled the way she shrank away when he'd treated her gunshot wound.

The very thought made him want to find Div and tear him apart.

"When I first spotted someone following me, I thought it was just part of my nightmares creeping into reality. Until it kept happening, and I would see the same person in different places I'd go, and then someone broke into my house. I packed up everything and fled, only somehow, they kept finding me…at least until I came to Montana. There hasn't been any sighting of this mystery creep in a few years now. I thought I was safe—thought Rose was safe."

He hated that she'd had to go through this alone. "I wish I'd known," he said quietly. Even with what Lee had been going through before her death, he would have found a way to help Jade.

Ethan remembered Jade talking about a boy she'd gone to school with. She'd planned to marry him once she returned from the war. "What happened with you and Stephen?"

Her eyes turned stormy, and she ducked her head. "It didn't work out." Those simple words held so much emotion. He understood how hard it was to settle back into civilian life under normal circumstances. He couldn't imagine what Jade had gone through living with trauma and having someone following her.

"I'm sorry," he murmured. The same words so many had said to him after Lee's passing seemed as inadequate now as they did back then.

"It's okay. It was for the best." Yet there was a catch in her voice that contradicted what she said.

"Is this why you traveled around so much? Because you were being followed?"

Her jaw tensed. Both hands balled into fists before she slowly relaxed. "Yes. I almost lost track of Rose completely." She grew quiet for a breath. "I knew I couldn't keep running. I had a friend in the FBI. When I reached out to him, he was able to arrange an interview here in Montana where Rose was attending university. I guess they were impressed with my service record because I was hired."

Ethan smiled at her humility. That was Jade. He'd gotten a call from a supervisor in Missoula, and he'd given her an excellent recommendation. Jade had been through enough. She deserved something tangible and a positive place to use her skills. The FBI was a good fit.

A rumbling beneath their feet yanked Ethan from the past. Vehicles were heading their way. He and Jade ducked behind a tree.

"I don't see anything," she murmured as she searched their snowy surroundings.

With the snow falling and the day fading, there wasn't any sunlight filtering through the trees. The woods were dark and shadowed. The vehicles would have to use lights to see better. "Why aren't they using lights?"

Ethan swung the backpack off his shoulder and removed his night-vision binoculars. He quickly panned the area where the rumbles came from. "I count at least four M1151 Enhanced Armament Carriers moving this way. They must be using the vehicle's guidance system to keep from crashing into the trees." He handed Jade the binoculars.

Those vehicles had an array of weapons on board including mounting and firing Mk 19 automatic grenade launchers; M2, M60 and M240 machine guns, and M249 squad automatic weapons. Enough to destroy a whole lot of things. If this was all Div's doing, he'd graduated from stealing weapons from battlefields to procuring far more powerful weaponry.

Ethan was worried about his friends. Had he sent Fletcher and Mason into a dangerous situation that might end in death? There was so much about what was happening he didn't understand.

The number of vehicles converging on this corner of the community seemed to speak of some imminent threat. The only questions were what was in the works and why hadn't the threat been picked up on before now?

The possibilities were as disturbing as the vehicles heading their way.

If equipped with infrared as Ethan was certain they would be, then these trees wouldn't hide either him or Jade for long. They couldn't afford to remain here any longer. The disturbing thought had barely cleared his head when the lead vehicle stopped. They were too late.

"Run, Jade!" Together, they ran for their lives, and all the while she knew they couldn't outrun the weapons coming their way for long.

They'd barely covered a few yards when the first vehicle started shooting at them.

The ground shook beneath their feet as more rounds were fired. Jade hit the ground. Ethan dropped beside her.

How were they going to get out of this?

"We've got to move," Ethan yelled above the sound of battle.

He was right. They'd die if they didn't move fast.

Jade lifted her head. There was a thicket of trees ahead growing far too closely together for the vehicles to enter. If they could make it there…

She pointed to the trees.

Ethan didn't hesitate. "On the three count."

Jade held his eyes and waited for three. When he reached it, they leapt to their feet and ran.

Her heartbeat jackhammered in her chest. Jade expected to be shot at any minute. The trees they were aiming for seemed miles away under these conditions.

The sound of a second round of shots pierced through the horrifying thoughts in her head.

"Stay low!" She became aware of Ethan yelling.

Jade ducked as low as she could while still remaining upright. With her breaths coming quickly, they finally reached the dense woods.

"Don't stop," Ethan told her, and she didn't.

They kept going while keeping low. The shooting continued all around.

Where had the dogs gone? With her breath burning in her chest, Jade glanced over her shoulder. She couldn't see anything, but by now the vehicles would have reached the thicket.

Ethan moved closer to her side. "They'll send others after us." His assumption matched her own. "This way." He veered farther to the right. After what felt like forever, they stopped long enough to catch their breaths.

Ethan used binoculars to check the enemy's location. "So far, they haven't picked up our change of direction. That won't last. Let's keep going." She observed him pull in a couple of breaths before they began walking at a fast pace.

"What about the dogs?" Jade was worried about the animals being harmed.

"They'll catch up with us. Molly is a combat dog. She'll know how to get away, and she'll help the others."

If they kept going in this direction, they'd lose Rose's scent. Hopefully, they could find it again once it was safe to resume the search.

Her heart continued to pound out a frantic rhythm in her ears.

"I don't see any signs of them. Strange. There's no way they'd give up." Ethan frowned as he panned the binoculars all around the area.

"Wait, there's the dogs." He pointed toward the animals bounding their way.

Jade had met the German shepherd, Molly, while working on Bowman's case.

"For now, we'll have to call off the search for Rose." Ethan checked the dogs to make sure they weren't injured before they started walking again.

Jade tried her phone and wasn't surprised that there was no service. "Do you think Fletcher and Mason are okay?" The two had been heading in the same direction that the vehicles had come from.

"Mason knows how to stay hidden." She wondered if he was trying to assure himself as much as her.

Lord, keep them safe... If she had brought her friends up to this mountain and gotten Mason and Fletcher hurt—or worse, she couldn't say the word—she would regret it for the rest of her life.

"This isn't in keeping with Div's MO. He's changed, and he's definitely planning something." She spoke her worst fears aloud.

Ethan met her gaze. "You're right. His organization has obviously grown, or more likely he's working with someone with a whole lot of money and enough power to get weapons and military vehicles into the country without question. There's no way they'd be moving so much heavy weaponry into this remote area if they weren't planning something major. Probably some type of national threat."

Hearing him say the words aloud sent a chill down her spine. If Div had joined forces with someone with a whole lot of money and a desire to destroy the US, then there would be no limit to what they were capable of doing.

FIVE

The amount of weaponry moving through such a remote mountain area was disturbing. Ethan hadn't seen as much since his days in Afghanistan, and the question foremost in his mind was where were those weapons heading and to what end?

One thing he knew for certain—whatever was happening here wasn't connected to the military, and the National Guard had never done maneuvers in this area.

Lord, we sure could use Your help figuring this out. The prayer slipped through his head as naturally as breathing, even though it wasn't always that way. Throughout adulthood, he'd gotten so far away from the faith of his childhood. Until he'd lost Lee. Her death had brought him to his knees and had him begging God for help. He couldn't imagine getting through the loss without having God's peace to sustain him.

"How far are we from the location where those weapons were being moved into the country?" he asked while trying to make sense of what was happening.

"I beg your pardon?" Jade jerked toward him. She'd been caught up in her own thoughts, much like him. After multiple attacks in a short amount of time, he could certainly understand her being on edge. Not to mention she was worried about her sister.

He repeated the question, and her expression cleared.

"I'd say as the crow flies maybe five miles, give or take." She glanced around at their surroundings. "There has to be an easier way to get those armored vehicles to wherever they're going than this. I know they're designed to cover all sorts of terrain, but coming up this way through the woods and the extreme mountain elevation doesn't seem like the smartest thing."

She made a good point, but... "They wouldn't be using this route if there was any other way. My guess is they want to keep their actions secret for as long as possible. I'm sure they have someone at the border who's been bought off to look the other way, but that only guarantees safe passage across the Canadian border. Once they're here on US soil, they have to stay out of sight."

Jade chewed on her bottom lip. "I get that, but where are they taking all these military vehicles?"

Ethan turned and looked in the direction they'd come, half-expecting to see those vehicles. "I wish I knew. Right now, let's focus on getting Rose back. Once she's safe, we'll work on figuring out what's really happening here." He nodded toward the dogs. "They appear to be back on track." The last thing he wanted was another run-in with those tanks. The outcome could have been far worse.

He and Jade followed the dogs. "Tell me everything you remember about Div's meeting with Bowman that led you to following his associates to the border."

Her mouth thinned. "I guess you could say it was the only good thing to come from Zeke Bowman's rampage... I couldn't believe he was here in the US, but I knew that if he was, something bad was in the works. His call earlier only confirmed it's really him." She visibly shivered.

He couldn't imagine how terrifying it was to realize the one who had caused her so much pain was here in Montana. Ethan wished she'd trusted him enough to ask for help.

"Anyway, after I first thought that the man Zeke Bowman had met with at the ranch was the same terrorist I knew as Div, I had to find out why he was here. After Bowman was arrested, Rose and I went back to the ranch and staked it out. It paid off big time. Rose and I followed an SUV at a safe distance and arrived at a location that was close to the Canadian border where there were other vehicles waiting. As soon as the vehicles arrived, people waiting at the site moved quickly to load several large containers into each of the SUVs, but get this—they didn't load everything from the other vehicles."

Ethan frowned. "They were splitting the load up for a reason."

Jade nodded. "That would be my guess. I'm thinking they're moving the weapons to different strategic locations."

Ethan ran his hand across his weary eyes. He'd been out of the war games for a long time; still, it was hard to make sense of how such massive amounts of weapons had gotten to this point in the US—even with the help of some dirty border patrol agents—without being detected.

"I sure hope Mason and Fletcher were able to reach Walker." His gut told him it would be only a matter of time before those military vehicles located him and Jade again. And this time, they'd probably bring backup. Because whatever was in the works here was far too important to let Jade and Ethan stand in the way of whatever was in the works.

"How long do you think they'll keep her alive?" Jade's question brought him back to their immediate concern. Unraveling what Div had planned was important, but getting Rose away from Div before he decided she was no longer of any use to his cause was critical. Playing the what-if game wouldn't serve a purpose, and it would only torture Jade.

"Don't go there. The dogs appear to be on Rose's trail. We'll find her."

She forced a smile. "You're right, I know. I have to stay positive."

He noticed her holding her side. "How's that holding up?" Ethan pointed to it when she raised her brows.

"I'm okay." The strain on her face spoke differently. As much as he wished they could stop to rest, Molly and the team were relentlessly hunting Rose.

The ground rumbled beneath their feet, and Jade jerked toward the source of the sound. "They're coming after us."

Ethan gave a short whistle to call the dogs off the hunt for now. Getting out of sight was imperative. "Over there." He and Jade took cover, but with the technology that came equipped on the military vehicles, they wouldn't be able to stay hidden for long.

Ethan leaned over enough to see the lead vehicle roll to a stop. Soon the vehicle emptied of combatants.

"Find them." A voice could be heard over the noise of the machines. "We can't let them escape again."

"We have to get out of here now," Jade whispered.

If they stayed, they'd be found and forced into a shootout and possibly killed. Right now, Ethan still believed they needed Jade and were using Rose to get her to talk.

"Over there." A different voice confirmed Ethan and Jade's location.

Ethan fired several times, forcing the advancing troops to seek cover.

"Let's get out of here." He headed away from the attack with Jade in front of him with the dogs. Several shooters zeroed in and opened fire.

"Stay low!" Ethan yelled as bullets whizzed by. Ducking for cover, he realized if they stayed in one place it would all but guarantee they'd be captured. "Go ahead of me with the dogs, and I'll cover you."

She was close enough for him to see all her fear. "They'll kill you."

He did his best to assure her he'd be okay, while trying to keep the fiercely protective Molly and her fellow SAR dogs from charging after their assailants to their deaths. He was counting on the Shetlers to reach the sheriff and bring help. "Take the dogs." She held his gaze while emotions he couldn't begin to explain had him hesitating. The noise of footsteps moving through the woods had him dragging his attention away from her. "Go. Hurry, Jade."

Ethan gave the command for the dogs to run. With a final searching look his way, Jade ran after the animals while Ethan covered her and hoped to draw attention away from her escape.

Several shooters returned fire, splintering off pieces of the tree where Ethan hid. He dove for the next one. The enemy's search appeared to be taking place entirely on foot, which gave him and Jade a small advantage. He knew the woods better than their attackers.

If he could get Div's goons to think they'd changed direction then he and Jade had a chance.

Bullets flew all around. Several far too close. He couldn't stay here. While he prepared to run for the next tree, an eerie silence followed. Had he done enough to take the shooters' attention off Jade and make them believe they were headed north? Ethan sure hoped so.

Pulling in a breath, he took off running, half-expecting to be mowed down. When the onslaught didn't come, he grabbed the backpack he'd shucked and ran in the direction Jade had fled. After covering some distance, Ethan pulled out the binoculars and searched the space behind him for any signs of Div's men or the armored vehicles. So far, nothing.

Ethan drew a couple of breaths and kept going. Behind him, it sounded as if the military vehicles were on the move. He couldn't tell the direction. Was it his imagination or were the tanks moving away? Nothing about that made sense unless…they'd radioed for backup to this location. Foot soldiers to search for him and Jade.

With not a second to spare, Ethan hit a trot and ran through the woods. A sound close by had him jerking toward it with his weapon drawn. Before he could squeeze the trigger, he got a better look and realized it was Jade. She had her weapon aimed at him as well.

"Oh, wow," he muttered and quickly lowered the weapon while doubling over with relief.

If they'd reacted a second slower, both might have died by their own hands.

"Ethan, I could have killed you," Jade whispered while her unsteady hand tucked the weapon inside her jacket. "What happened? I heard shooting."

"I'll explain as we walk." They headed in the direction Jade had been going when she'd heard Ethan coming.

He explained about the military vehicles leaving the area. "I've no doubt they've radioed others to take up the search. We're by no means out of danger, but they're being called off for a reason." Ethan's eyes zeroed in on hers. "This is serious, Jade."

"There has to be a target nearby that Div plans to attack." She searched her mind to recall any military base, or perhaps a building that might be considered symbolic enough to be a target. Nothing stood out. "Maybe they're moving the vehicles out of Montana?"

"Possibly. Still, I don't see the purpose of armored vehicles. They'd need a whole lot more to make any impact unless..." He stopped walking.

"Unless what?" She stared at him.

"The vehicles are equipped with something that will cause a lot of destruction like..."

"Some type of nuclear weapons," Jade finished for him as a sinking feeling took hold of her. "Oh, Ethan, this is bad."

He nodded. "We have to find a way to let your assistant director know what's happening."

But how? Cell service was affected by the weather.

The dogs kept their noses to the ground as they moved through the dense underbrush. So far, there was no indication that more of Div's troops had found their location, but it was only a matter of time before they were pinpointed.

Ethan gestured to the dogs. "They're definitely on the scent."

Jade assessed the direction they were headed. If they kept on the current trajectory, they'd be heading straight toward the Canadian border. She told Ethan as much.

"Would they take Rose back to the location where she was captured?"

It didn't seem like a wise choice in her opinion. "You're right, it doesn't make sense."

"Unless they're not going back to that location but someplace else."

"The ranch!" she exclaimed. "Maybe Div is taking her to the ranch where he met up with Bowman?"

"I guess it's possible, but it seems like a bad move. You knew about it, and he has no way of knowing you didn't report it to the FBI." Ethan shook his head. "For now, we follow the scent. Keep your eyes open. We have no idea how many others might be combing these woods. I'm going to try Walker again."

Ethan grabbed his phone and placed the call before shaking his head. "This weather's still jamming the signal. Let's hope the GPS beacons on the dogs' collars are working properly. We sure could use some help."

He'd told her once that the GPS signals in the dogs' collars allowed for not only their handler but also for others on the SAR team to track their location if needed. It became an invaluable tool when the handler lost contact with the base location.

Would the signals be the one thing to save their lives?

The temperature seemed to be plummeting with the approaching nightfall.

While her thoughts ping-ponged between fearing for Rose's safety and trying to understand what Div had planned, the dogs suddenly stopped and sniffed around. "They've lost the scent."

Ethan's jaw tightened. "It's the snow. It's coming in too fast."

"What do we do?" Without a scent, they were wandering around the woods without a clue which direction to go.

Ethan glanced up at the skies, which had begun to darken, while snow covered his upturned face. "For now, we need to find a place to take cover and warm up. We're in danger of hypothermia setting in otherwise. Let's wait for the brunt of the snowstorm to pass. Right now, we appear to be safe enough." When she would have protested, he added, "If we're struggling with the weather, so will they."

She prayed the time lost wouldn't result in Div moving Rose out of the area.

As much as Jade wished for a place to get out of the snowstorm, she and Ethan were up on the mountain without any place to seek shelter. "What I wouldn't give for an abandoned cabin, or even an old barn."

Ethan's smile softened the strain around his eyes. "You might get your wish. Believe it or not, there are several hunting cabins up here. My friend Aaron—Mason and Fletcher's older brother—told me that in the past they provided shelter from the weather for hunters and acted as a base camp while trappers worked during the winter months."

"Really? That's good to hear."

Twilight made it hard to see much beyond a few feet. Jade's foot struck a downed tree branch covered in snow, and her ankle twisted. She would have gone down if Ethan hadn't reached for her waist to steady her.

She tensed immediately and Ethan felt it and let her go. He was only trying to help, she told herself, and yet… She stopped and took the weight off her injured leg. It broke her that a simple gesture of kindness sent her back to the past and that terrible night, almost reducing her to a shivering and frightened mess. Still today, after so long, she'd wake up in the middle of the night in a cold sweat screaming because in her nightmare she was right back in Afghanistan with a monster.

Jade clamped down on her bottom lip to keep from crying. She'd worked so hard to overcome the pain of losing her parents. Joining the military had been good. It had made her stronger and self-confident until…

"Are you okay?" Ethan asked, his attention trained on her face, probably seeing all sorts of things she wished she could keep to herself.

"I will be," she managed to get out.

"Can you walk?"

"I think so." Yet the second she put pressure on her foot, the pain was excruciating.

"Let me help. I'm going to put my arm around your waist to help take some of the pressure off your ankle." He was warning her of what he planned to do so as to not surprise her. Jade was torn between immense gratitude and heartbreaking regret that she was still so damaged.

"Are you ready?" Ethan asked gently.

Jade gathered herself and nodded. "I'm ready."

He stepped close and put his arm carefully

around her waist. "We'll go slowly. As soon as we can find a place out of the weather, I'll look at your ankle."

Ethan helped take some of the weight off her ankle, but she couldn't keep going like this for long.

"I once came up here to do some exploring," he said quietly, his breath brushing against her temple.

Jade closed her eyes. "Why?" She asked the first question that came to mind while her voice shook a little. Was this strong reaction all because of her aversion to being touched, or her response to being close to Ethan? She wasn't so sure.

Ethan hesitated long enough to draw her attention to his face.

"It was after my wife died," he said at last. "I felt so lost back then that I didn't know what to do with myself."

Jade remembered how horrible she'd felt for him after hearing the news of his wife's passing. "I'm so sorry," she whispered.

"Thank you," he whispered in a rough voice.

Their eyes met and held. His arm around her didn't evoke the usual repulsion. Ethan's touch was different. Jade's chest tightened painfully, and she struggled to get enough air into her lungs.

"I explored every inch of this mountain back then. That's why I'm pretty sure there is a small shelter not too far ahead of us."

As she continued to watch him, Jade realized he was telling her something. "I'm sorry?" She forced the words out.

"We should keep going." His voice sounded as unsteady as hers. Did he feel the same reaction to their closeness?

Slowly, they made their way along with the dogs.

Jade prayed the storm would pass quickly and the K9s would be able to pick up Rose's trail again, because the clock was ticking on her life.

SIX

In the dying light of day, Ethan desperately searched for the cabin. His legs felt as if they were weighed down. Picking up his feet proved nearly impossible. They were in danger from the elements and needed to find shelter quickly. He should have found the cabin by now. What if he'd gotten off course by just a little? The thought was crushing. If they didn't find shelter soon, they'd both succumb to the weather.

Jade was struggling, and they both could use a break.

He'd been so certain the cabin was just beyond that group of trees...

"What's wrong?" Jade asked as if sensing his turmoil.

"Nothing... I'm not sure." They kept going.

"Are we getting close?" she asked.

He didn't want her to give up. "I believe so." Yet nothing could be further from the truth.

"The snow is really deep up here," Jade whispered in a weak tone. She was fading quickly.

He stopped abruptly and grabbed the binoculars. "I see something." He pointed ahead. "There. That's the cabin."

"Oh, thank goodness."

Jade leaned heavily against him, likely as the pain in her ankle became more intense.

Ethan slowly moved through the snow with her until they were standing in front of the door.

The growing darkness made it hard to see much. He brought out his flashlight and panned around the ground. "I don't see any footprints." He turned her way. "Let's get inside."

Ethan shoved against the door with all his weight until it finally gave way. Together, they stepped into the single-room cabin devoid of luxuries. There was a small table and a couple of chairs along with a woodstove in the corner. Jade's attention lingered on the stove. He'd give just about anything to be able to have a fire, but it would be drawing the enemy straight to their location.

Ethan helped her over to one of the chairs while the dogs roamed around the space. Then he placed a second chair in front of Jade. "Let's elevate your leg for now." He gently lifted it up to the chair and removed her boot. Though swollen, the sprain wasn't so bad. "I'll secure it as tight as you can stand, and we'll keep the pressure off for a bit."

"How long do you think before the storm lifts?"

He worked quickly to wrap the ankle, noticing her gripping the chair in discomfort.

"Hopefully, not long. Sorry, I know it hurts but that should make it better," Ethan said once he'd finished. He walked to the window and looked out. Every second they weren't on the move they risked being discovered, but Jade needed rest.

He turned from the window. "I have some aspirin in my bag. It should help take the edge off the pain."

He rummaged through his bag until he found the pills and then handed her one and a bottle of water.

"Thank you." She popped the aspirin in her mouth and washed it down.

Ethan placed his backpack against the wall near the door and then sat down on the table's edge.

"I really was sorry to hear about your wife," Jade told him quietly. "I can't imagine how hard that was for you."

He lifted his head. At times, when he'd wake up from a sweet dream of her, Lee's image would disappear, and he would struggle to remember what she looked like. He believed that was the real reason he'd kept her photos scattered around the house. If he lost what she looked like, then he'd forget all the years of sacrifice Lee had given to the Marines as well.

He couldn't let her sacrifice be in vain.

Come home, Ethan...

Every time he thought about that last phone conversation he'd had with Lee before he'd returned home to Montana, that little catch in her voice ripped his heart to pieces.

"I got your letter. It meant a lot."

Through all the times they'd been together recently, they'd never really talked about what happened to Jade in Afghanistan or about Lee.

Ethan listened above the sounds of the storm blowing through for anything else.

She slowly raised her face to him. "I'm the reason my relationship with Stephen didn't work out. Since I came home, well, things have been hard. I haven't been able to fit into life again."

His heart went out to her. Ethan had wondered if that might have been the reason for their breakup.

"You've joined the FBI now. It looks as if you've found your place."

"I enjoy the work. It was interesting being undercover with Bowman's organization. I learned a lot about the criminal mind." She shook her head.

"Bowman's a lightweight compared to what is going on here."

She visibly shivered. "I'm worried, Ethan. What if we can't find Rose? What if we can't stop Div in time?"

The fear on her face reminded Ethan of the power Div still held over her.

"I know you're scared, but you can't give in to it, Jade," he said gently. "I firmly believe we're going to find Rose. We're going to stop Div." He glanced down at her foot. "How's your ankle feeling?"

"Much better, thank you. Do you think the storm has let up enough to start out again?" Jade grabbed her boot and slipped it on.

Ethan glanced toward the grimy window. The growing darkness made it hard to see anything. "Let me take a look around outside. Stay here and rest." He took Molly with him and left the two younger dogs. Before following Molly out into the twilight, he checked his handgun's magazine. It wouldn't do to get caught out alone with limited ammunition.

The cold was a shock to his system. Though he wore a knit cap, it seemed as if the temperatures had dropped drastically since they'd been inside. Ethan raised the hood on his jacket for added protection against the elements. The snow appeared to be letting up at least. Still, he worried that with what had accumulated, it would be nearly impossible for the dogs to pick up the tracks again.

If they couldn't find Rose's trail again, then there were thousands of acres of wilderness to cover, and if they didn't find the right direction soon, Div wouldn't think twice about getting rid of any witnesses.

Jade rose and tentatively tested her injured ankle. Nimshi and Trackr rousted themselves and came over to watch as she moved around the small cabin. Though she was still a long way from being pain free, the rest had helped.

She stopped in front of the window and rubbed her hands together for warmth. How long had Ethan been gone? Ten, maybe fifteen minutes. What if their pursuers had pinned him down out there? He could be in danger.

Jade started for the door when a shadow passed by the window. She ducked away. A second later, the door opened, and Ethan came inside.

Relief made her limbs weak.

Ethan looked around until he spotted her. "How is it?" He indicated the injured ankle.

"Better. It looks as if the snow is letting up somewhat."

He nodded. "We should keep moving. Hopefully, the dogs will be able to find Rose's scent again." Ethan picked up his backpack and shouldered it.

Jade once more removed Rose's coat and held it out to the dogs before they stepped outside. Molly and the two Saint Bernards charged from the cabin. "I just hope my wearing it won't tamper with Rose's scent."

"Looks like for now we're okay," Ethan said. The sight of the dogs on the hunt was encouraging. Not that Jade had a choice in wearing the coat. It was freezing out.

"Did you find any sign we were being followed?"

"Not that I could see, but best not to stay in one place too long."

She snuggled her jacket closer around her body against the biting chill. "Do you think Mason and Fletcher were able to reach the sheriff?"

He looked at her curiously. "I sure hope so."

Jade kept her attention on the dogs, who were still searching for their trail, while she thought about her relationship with Ethan. They'd known each other for a long time; first during her tour of duty in Afghanistan and then more recently when she'd helped rescue him from a drug smuggler's captivity. After Bowman was taken down, they'd grown closer. Both made a point to check on each other. She'd been to Ethan's ranch and participated in his training of the dogs, and he'd come to her house for dinner many times.

Jade had to admit she was seeing him differently. Not so much as her lieutenant, but as a friend. She found herself thinking a lot about him lately. In the Marines, he'd been her commander and married. She never thought about him as handsome…yet he was. Jade couldn't deny she was attracted to Ethan. But handsome or not, she had to deny the attraction she felt to him because she'd finally come to accept that she was best on her own. She had Rose. Best not to wish for things that couldn't be hers.

When she'd returned from Afghanistan, she was a different person. She hated letting anyone close—couldn't bear being touched. Stephen hadn't known how to make it better. In the end, it was just too hard to try to be the woman he wanted her to be, and so she'd ended their engagement. Jade had heard Stephen had gotten married a few years back.

Ethan stopped suddenly and stuck his arm out, barring her way.

Jade jerked toward him. Before she could get words out, he held his finger against his lips. A second later, she heard what had alerted him. Voices. Ethan leaned in closer. "It sounds like it's coming from down the mountain, still some distance from us."

The snow helped muffle their footsteps, but it would also lead the enemy to their location every step of the way.

Within seconds, the cold bored down deep. Breathing through the cold was difficult enough without the constant reminder of the injury to her side. She carefully picked her way along, favoring her injured ankle.

Jade checked the path behind them periodically. In darkness, it would be impossible to see the advancing troops until it was too late, and she doubted they'd risk using flashlights.

She spotted something on the ground and hobbled over to investigate. "It's a hair clip." Jade leaned closer. The type used by Rose… as well as countless others. "It could be my sister's." While she turned the item over in her hand, a crack reverberated through the woods.

Jade hit the ground next to Ethan. Someone was shooting at them.

Staying low, she and Ethan crawled to the nearest tree. Another round of shots followed.

"We can't stay here," she told him once silence settled.

Running would be a gamble with her injured ankle, but it was the only option. "They're probably reloading, so we won't have long." She counted off three seconds in her head and stumbled to her feet. Sticking close to her side, Ethan gave the order for the dogs to bolt. They reached the next group of trees before being forced to take cover again.

Jade inched up to a sitting position. "We won't be able to outrun them." Especially not with her ankle. There was only one way to survive this, and that was to pick off each of their assailants one by one. Jade realized the odds of her and Ethan being on the winning end of this gamble were minute.

"You're right." Ethan glanced around the space.

Their pursuers were probably using infrared technology. The only thing she and Ethan had going for them was that Div most likely needed her alive.

"If I can reach that group of trees, I can draw their fire away from you." Staying low, Ethan ran for his target.

She understood it would provide more of a challenge if they weren't together, yet she felt his absence the second he moved away. Shots rained down all around Ethan.

Jade screamed as the attack seemed to go on forever. The dogs were nowhere in sight. Had they gotten hit in the crossfire?

Ethan barely waited for another break in the

action before he scrambled to the next vantage point. Through the darkness and the distance, their gazes held. Her breath lodged in her throat. The man watching her was a true hero, and she felt something long dead. Jade was grateful she had Ethan to count on no matter what. He hadn't hesitated to come to her aid.

They'd been in this position many times in battle. The waiting was the hardest part. If their gamble had been correct, it was only a matter of time before the shooters came this way, and it was up to her and Ethan to survive.

Despite being through this before, it was never easy. Waiting to engage the enemy without knowing how many were coming meant being faced with a whole lot of unknowns.

She bit back a scream when footsteps crunched in the snow nearby. The first shooter was almost on top of her location. Jade indicated the person to Ethan, who gave a quick nod of confirmation.

Keeping her attention on the space between the trees, she waited for the first sign. A boot appeared. This was it. Once the person cleared the tree, she fired once. He dropped, his lifeless eyes staring up at Jade.

She grabbed the weapon from his hand and waited for the next perp to appear.

SEVEN

Several footsteps rushed toward their location. Ethan fired at the first perp, striking his shoulder.

"Ethan, watch out."

A second was right on top of him before he had time to react to Jade's warning. Ethan grabbed the attacker's shooting arm. The gun jerked, and a shot flew past Ethan's head.

Before Jade could render aid, she was forced to fight for her life.

Ethan slugged his attacker hard. He stumbled backward a few feet still holding the weapon. As he prepared to shoot, Ethan beat him to the draw and fired.

The attacker fell forward. Ethan was forced to wrestle the dead weight to the ground.

Jade struggled with her attackers. "Watch out!" Ethan called and raced to her aid. Two perps were engaged in hand-to-hand combat with her, making it hard to get a shot off without hitting Jade.

Someone grabbed Ethan's arm, knocking the weapon away. Another one of Div's goons wrapped his hands around Ethan's throat and tried to strangle him.

A shot rang out. Ethan squeezed his eyes shut, thinking he'd been hit. A breath later, Jade was pulling the dead guy off him.

While she struggled to remove the body, another assailant grabbed her and jerked her to her feet. The attacker slugged Jade hard. Before she had time to recover, he was on her.

Ethan leapt to his feet and yanked the attacker off Jade.

Another shot came from close by, and the assailant fell at Ethan's feet like a ragdoll. Ethan's gaze flew to where Jade still held in position the weapon that had made the kill shot. She'd saved his life again.

"Thank you," he murmured in an unsteady voice. Ethan grabbed the perps' weapons while half-expecting more to appear. "We should put as much space between us and these guys as possible." Because he didn't for a second believe they'd seen the last of Div's associates.

With Jade close, they started walking again. "Where are my dogs?" he asked, still trying to catch his breath.

"I don't know. I haven't seen them since the attack started."

As much as he wanted to use his flashlight to locate the animals, it would lead others straight to his and Jade's location.

Molly, Nimshi and Trackr were smart. They'd find their way back.

He leaned down and spotted the dogs' paw prints heading off to the right. "This way." As they followed the animals, Ethan's hands still shook as his mind recalled every detail of the attack they'd barely escaped. The enemy had been skilled, but not trained by the military. He told Jade as much.

"I agree. Still, those were some hand-to-hand skills. They gave us a run for our money. I'm guessing they are highly motivated to succeed, and I'm sure Div doesn't suffer failure well." She looked over her shoulder before adding, "The person who followed me in Alaska had the same caliber of training." She related how she'd been forced to fight for her life in order to escape.

Ethan thought about the person who had caused so much trouble. "Can you tell me more about the one who followed you to Alaska?"

Jade's mouth thinned. She clearly didn't like talking about what had happened.

"I know it's hard, but had you ever seen the person before?"

Jade was one of only two people who could

identify Div's voice. He'd eliminated one threat—Arezo.

"It wasn't Div if that's what you're thinking," she said, reading his thoughts. "I can't explain it but my instincts tell me it wasn't him, just someone working for him."

"Did he speak to you?" He wondered how she could be so certain the person following her was connected to Div's organization.

Jade shook her head. "No, never. And I probably wouldn't have thought anything of it if I hadn't seen the same guy at my previous location. He was clearly following me."

"So, you left?" He couldn't imagine how terrifying that must have been for Jade after everything she'd gone through in Afghanistan. To think that the person responsible was having her followed.

"Yes. That very day. He attacked me, but I managed to overpower him. I knocked him out and ran the entire way back to the small one-room cabin where I was staying. After I'd thrown everything I owned into my bag, I left the life I'd established there behind."

All these years, he'd been living his life—even after losing Lee, he'd been living his life expecting his past to come after him, only it hadn't. But for Jade it had.

Ethan struggled to make sense of Div's motives for keeping tabs on her. If she was such a threat, why not kill her while he'd had the opportunity? He considered what was happening now. The military vehicles had put a whole different spin on things. It catapulted Div into an entirely different category. He wasn't just a mild irritation as he'd been to the military in Afghanistan. If he had the capability to get his hands on military armored vehicles, then what else was he capable of obtaining?

"It was then that I returned to the Lower 48," Jade was saying. "Rose was finishing her education in Missoula, and so I came here and worked on repairing my damaged relationship with my sister. I later joined the FBI." She turned her head to him. "Thank you for the recommendation, by the way. I know they reached out to you."

He inclined his head. "It was well deserved."

She smiled and his heart did a little flip. He broke eye contact and noticed paw prints on the ground.

"The dogs have been through here. Let's catch up with them. The three have a head start on us, and they appear to be moving fast."

Jade bit her bottom lip and frowned. He wondered if she was even aware of the gesture he'd seen her make many times both recently and when they were in the war zone.

If the trail was still viable, Molly and the two Saint Bernard dogs would find it. But he was worried. Had all the snow buried whatever scent might still exist? If so, they could be walking around blindly with no idea where they were going and a virtual army searching for him and Jade.

Not showing the exhaustion swamping her body was nearly impossible. It made each step feel as if she were climbing an insurmountable mountain.

"There—I see the dogs." Ethan drew her attention back to the path ahead. The three animals appeared through the darkness. "It sure seems like they're on track."

"Thank You, God." Relief flooded her limbs. It was hard to get a sense of things with the darkness and the woods, but she was pretty sure they were heading toward the border area. Not the staging location she and Rose had followed the SUVs to.

The armored vehicles worried her. Though carrying a lot of firepower, their speed wasn't great. It would take the vehicles a while to reach their destination. Had Div been at this for years? She shared her concerns with Ethan.

"It's possible," he replied. "He could have camps set up around the countryside to keep the weapons and vehicles hidden before disbursing them to their target location. It would be easy enough in these woods and unlikely someone would happen upon the camp."

They were missing the big picture. "If Div has managed to get military tanks across the border to different locations across the US, possibly with nuclear weapons attached to the tanks, then the damage would be widespread and bring the country to its knees."

"You're right, and we can't let that happen. We've got to stop him." Ethan whistled for the dogs to hold up. "Let's take a breather. I can tell your ankle is giving you grief."

She smiled gratefully. "Thank you." She found a downed tree trunk and dusted off the snow.

Ethan sat beside her and removed his backpack. He opened it, took out two waters and handed her one.

The water tasted wonderful, and she drank deep.

Jade pulled her phone out of her pocket. "No signal. We won't be able to let the sheriff and his deputies know where we are." She turned troubled eyes to Ethan.

"Walker will know I'd bring along the dogs. He'll use their GPS to locate us."

She wanted to believe it. Imagining they were

up here searching for Rose and no one knew where they were was terrifying.

"We'll be okay," he told her as if reading her thoughts.

She smiled. "I don't think I've told you how much I appreciate you coming after me, Ethan. I know you've risked your life, and I really appreciate it."

"Are you kidding? I owe you. If you hadn't done what you did with Bowman, I'd be dead for sure. Not to mention you just saved my life again."

Ethan was the type of man who didn't like to take credit for doing the right thing. It was just who he was. She'd seen it often during her time serving under him. Ethan was a protector and looked after his unit and their needs above his own.

"Did you notice the number of people who were at the staging camp?" Ethan asked.

"Probably ten or more. And I'd say there were two or three in each of the five vehicles. They didn't waste time either. Once the SUVs were on site, some of the containers were loaded inside and then all of the vehicles split up."

"You and Rose followed the SUVs that left?"

She nodded. "Some, anyway. I wanted to see if any of the SUVs would return to the ranch."

"And did they?"

"Yes. We sat on it for a while, but there was no movement. Rose and I were forced to abandon the stakeout for the time being."

"But you went back?" he concluded because he knew her.

"We did. There was no sign of the SUVs again. I think Div knew we were watching and waited until we'd left to move them." She blew out a breath. "But I had a feeling there would be more shipments going to the staging location after crossing the border, and so Rose and I went back."

She had his full attention. "What did you find?"

Her eyes turned dark. "That was the most concerning. Ethan, there were at least half a dozen different vehicles being loaded by people dressed in camo. What we'd witnessed before definitely wasn't an isolated incident. Div's been moving weapons into the country for months or longer." She looked him in the eye. "Maybe even years."

Ethan's reaction was just as grim as hers. "If that's the case, there could be militants already in place and who knows how much weaponry around the country waiting for the word to start a coordinated attack. This is bad, Jade. So bad. We've got to get help to stop this attack from happening."

Jade had made a huge mistake in not reporting the incident to her superiors right away. At the time, she'd wanted to gather more intel on Div's organization for her assistant director because she didn't want her team to think she was tracking Div for revenge. Though that was the real reason—she wanted to make Div pay for what he'd done to her and to Arezo. If her team were brought in, that chance would be taken from her. She and Rose had been compiling photos and documenting movements since they'd followed the SUVs to the location. Still, she'd wondered if it was enough. She hadn't been able to get close enough to see inside the containers. Without solid proof, Jade was working on conjecture alone. That was why she'd taken the risk of getting closer, but it hadn't worked, and it had almost cost them both dearly.

"We needed proof. I told Rose to wait for me near our vehicle. I wanted to get a better look."

Ethan watched her carefully. "Something happened."

"Yes. I went in dark. The property was cluttered with debris from previous owners. When Rose made a sound, I was so afraid we were caught." She blew out a breath. "We managed to get away, but just barely."

"Did you come back?"

"Yes, the following day. Everything was gone,

and the place was almost spotless. They made sure there was nothing left behind to incriminate them. Div won't go back there. The location is compromised."

Ethan's jaw flexed. "And I'm sure they told Div what they saw."

That was probably how Div had known it was her, or had he been keeping track of her all this time without her knowing about it?

Had her stubbornness to take Div down sealed Rose's fate?

EIGHT

The quiet of the woods was interrupted only by their careful footsteps. Even the dogs moving through the underbrush made little more than a background sound.

A temporary reprieve. Yet not for a second did he believe he and Jade had seen the last of Div's mercenaries. There were more out there. Staying alert meant surviving.

Once they reached the mountaintop, Ethan spotted something in the valley below that was disturbing. "Is that a light?"

Jade stepped close and focused on where he pointed. "It is. Several, in fact." She looked over at him. "Could be where they're holding Rose?"

A little too convenient in Ethan's opinion. He removed his backpack and brought out the binoculars. "There are several buildings. The lights we're seeing are from one building in particular." He handed her the binoculars.

"I don't see anyone around." She lowered the

binoculars. "It could be a warehouse of some sort. Maybe they keep the lights on to discourage trespassing."

"Probably."

Jade handed him back the binoculars, and he focused on the dogs moving downhill. "They're heading straight for the camp. I'd say that's a good sign. Let's see what's going on."

The steep downhill grade made every step perilous. Finding the right footing became a matter of life and death.

"Maybe I should go down alone. I'll check it out and then come back for you."

He barely finished speaking before she rejected the idea. "No, Ethan, no. We're in this together. I know you're trying to protect me, but don't. I can handle myself."

He'd always been overprotective of her, but after everything Jade had gone through, the thought of Div hurting her again was unacceptable. Ethan cared about her... As soon as the thought popped into his head it had him examining his feelings. Jade was one of his own, and he wanted to help her because of it. That was all it was. His heart wouldn't let him go below the surface of that reasoning. What if he let Jade into his heart, and he let her down? What if his failures returned, and Jade ended up getting hurt, or worse—dying?

"You're right," he murmured without looking at her. They started downhill carefully. Ethan stopped periodically to check the path they'd come down. So far, there was no sign of anyone.

At ground level, the camp was still some distance away. Both he and Jade remained on edge, their weapons drawn and ready to fire if needed. Even the dogs seemed to pick up on the tension.

When they reached the edge of the camp, Ethan stopped the K9s and panned the binoculars around the camp. "I don't see anyone, but we can't be too careful. Stay close to me and keep your eyes open."

He kept the dogs at his side as they entered the encampment, which consisted of five different outbuildings all in various sizes and stages of decay. The light burning near one of the buildings assured him someone had kept up with the utilities, but the rotting structures made him wonder if they would find anything living here.

"Heel." Ethan waited for the dogs to obey the command before approaching the first building. The hair on the back of his neck stood at attention. What if they were walking into a trap?

With his eyes sending a silent warning to Jade, Ethan grabbed the door handle and turned it. The door didn't budge. Years of harsh winter weather had it practically glued to the frame. Ethan threw his full weight against it, and it finally gave way.

It took time for his eyes to adjust to the darkness. The windowless building proved devoid of anything human. Ethan flipped on the flashlight and searched the room. Nothing there but years of dust.

"Wait, I see something over there." Jade pointed to the floor. Imprinted in the dust were several sets of footprints. "Someone's been here recently."

Ethan noticed that something appeared to have been stored in the corner at one time. "And kept something as well." He glanced back at Jade. "Let's check the rest of the camp. If they held Rose here at one time, the dogs will pick up her scent."

Outside, Molly, Trackr and Nimshi waited where he'd left them.

Jade held the jacket out to the dogs. "With all the weather the jacket has gone through, not to mention me wearing it, I hope there's still enough scent left to be useful."

It wasn't long before the three stuck their noses to the ground. Soon, Trackr and Nimshi picked up a scent. Molly followed their lead for once.

Jade shot Ethan a look as they rushed after the dogs. "She's been here at one time."

All three animals stopped in front of the illuminated building. Ethan worried what they'd find inside. Before he could caution her to wait outside, Jade had the door open. The dogs raced in first and headed straight for a single chair—the only piece of furniture in the room.

Several pieces of rope lay near the chair. "She was tied up."

Jade quickly searched the rest of the space. "There's more signs that something was stored here." She blew out a breath. "Do you have any idea where we are?"

Ethan's gut twisted. He was all too familiar with the area. At one time, Lee's father had a spread here. He'd worked as a rancher for years. Al was the reason Ethan and Lee had chosen to live in West Kootenai. They wanted to be close enough to visit Al whenever they wanted.

They'd planned to be there for Al in his senior years, but Lee had passed before her father. Al had died a few months after Lee, a broken man without his only child. "We're near Libby," he murmured with a catch in his voice. He'd done so many things wrong with Lee. He should have come home when she'd asked him to. If he had, they might have had more precious years together and not the six months that were filled with doctors' appointments, chemo and radiation treatments. Instead, he'd been fighting a war that was never won. Lee had been gone for more than five years now, and yet he still couldn't let go of the guilt.

He cleared his throat. "I'd say we're about

thirty miles from the border location where you and Rose first spotted the weapons."

Jade's frown deepened. "Some of the weapons must have been stored here at one time… and then what?"

That was the scary part. Whatever had been here at this camp could have been one of the most recent shipments or one from who knew how long ago.

Ethan tried to make a call again without any success. "Still nothing. We'll check the place, but I'm pretty sure we won't find anything useful here."

As they stepped out into the center of the camp once more, movement in the direction they'd come grabbed his attention. "We have company."

Half a dozen flashlights moved toward the camp. Jade whipped toward Ethan. "They're coming. We've gotta get out of here." With the dogs close, she and Ethan headed away from the lights. There was just enough time to duck behind one of the buildings to avoid being spotted by the lights. Unfortunately, there was no disguising their footprints.

"Someone's been here." A male voice carried their way. "Fan out. Find them."

Ethan flattened himself against the decaying walls and peeked out enough to see what was happening. "There are plenty coming," he whispered near Jade's ear.

Their only chance of escaping was to reach the woods without being spotted. Before she voiced her thoughts to Ethan, several of the lights reached the building ahead of them and were coming their way. The woods were no longer an option.

Jade kept her attention on the lights. "We'll have to make a run for it." She thought about her sprained ankle. Moving at all was painful, but there wasn't a choice. If they wanted to live, she'd have to ignore the pain. With a command from Ethan, the dogs glued themselves to his and Jade's side as they stepped from the partial safety of the building walls and into the open space.

Ethan pointed up ahead to the edge of the camp and tree coverage. "Head that way. Whatever you do, don't stop. Not even if we get separated."

He was warning her not to wait for him should that happen, but how could she leave him behind?

Jade ran toward the building closest to the woods while her heart pelted out a frantic beat that was so loud in her ears she could no longer hear anything around her.

"I see them. Hurry, they're getting away!" a different person yelled. Several flashlight beams immediately trained on Jade and Ethan.

"Run, Jade. Keep going."

She ran faster for the cover of the last building. Steps away from safety, an onslaught of bullets flew past.

"Get down!" Jade yelled over the noise of battle. Bending almost double, she and Ethan reached the building. Shots peppered the place they'd been standing seconds earlier.

"Don't stop," Ethan urged her on.

Once they reached the forested area, Jade felt somewhat less exposed, but they were far from being out of danger. Her arms pumped at her sides as she ran. Each breath burned her lungs. Beyond the camp, a road had been carved from the woods just wide enough for a vehicle to drive down. This had to be how they'd moved Rose and possibly the weapons.

"We can't use the road." She heard Ethan pull in several ragged breaths. "The enemy will be expecting it, and they're far too close to us right now. Over there." He indicated the dense wilderness to the right, and she started for it.

Since hiding their footprints wasn't an option, they'd have to outrun or outsmart their enemy.

The dogs quickly overtook Jade to lead the way. She couldn't see much beyond the three, but Jade used the animals for guidance.

A terrifying sound came from behind. Their pursuers had entered the woods.

"Fan out. They've come this way." The order was given. Like it or not, she and Ethan had to keep pushing on.

"How are you holding up?" Ethan whispered once he'd caught up with her.

She shook her head because words weren't possible. Her energy level was nearing the end.

Moving deeper into the woods, the trees and underbrush grew so close together it was difficult to move. "At least it will make it harder to find us."

Thankfully, the snow wasn't nearly as deep here.

After walking at a fast pace for some time, Jade peered over her shoulder. "I don't see the lights anymore."

Ethan focused on the dark space. "Me neither. Let's slow down a little."

Soon, her breathing returned to normal. "We need to get back to the road so we can use it for guidance. Div would have moved Rose by vehicle. He'd have to use the road."

"You're right." Ethan signaled the dogs to follow. Keeping a wide berth in case their attackers were in pursuit, he started back to the road.

Jade noticed the flashlights once more. "Over there." So far, the perps didn't seem to have picked up the change of direction.

As they walked, Jade struggled to fit together

the pieces of what they knew so far. Div's goons had taken Rose and brought her to the place they'd just left. Probably waiting for word Jade had been kidnapped. "By now, Div has to know I escaped. I'm guessing that's why he moved Rose. He knows we're looking for her."

Ethan's attention returned to her. "No doubt. There's the road up ahead."

They reached it and stared down both ways.

"Tire tracks. Someone's been down it recently." Jade's gaze followed the deep ruts left in the snow.

Keeping inside the tree coverage, she and Ethan began walking parallel to the road. Jade's concern over what Div and whoever he might be working with had planned continued to escalate. How long had he been smuggling weapons into the country? The organized way the containers had been moved from the staging camp spoke of a precise routine that had probably been happening for a while. This certainly wasn't the first time they'd done this. And that was the most disturbing aspect of all this. Div could have massive amounts of weapons stashed around the country just waiting for the right instant to signal an attack.

NINE

The woods appeared to be saturated with enemy troops. One false move could land Ethan and Jade square in the crosshairs of another attack.

Ethan was on edge and had been since he'd gotten the call from Jade—if he were being honest, he had been since he'd been kidnapped from his home along with Tanner Mast. They'd both almost died, and it still weighed heavily on his mind. He'd defeated death multiple times during the war and had almost died at the hands of Zeke Bowman recently—how many more second chances did he have left?

Ethan struggled to shake off the doubts. In the middle of a battle was no place to second-guess oneself. Both Jade and Rose were counting on him.

"Can we stop for a second?" Jade asked. He turned his head her way. For a while, she'd been heavily favoring her injured ankle.

"Good idea. Take the pressure off your ankle for a little while."

So far, there hadn't been any sign of the men from the camp, yet Ethan believed standing still for long was a liability.

Jade sank down to the ground without answering, further evidence that she was running on empty.

Ethan removed his backpack and dropped down beside her.

"Do you have any idea where this path will lead us?" she asked.

Ethan studied their surroundings. "There's another summit and then a wide valley. Eventually it will take us to Eagle's Nest, but that's a good twenty miles of hard walking."

Ethan kept his attention on her face. She appeared to be struggling to keep from falling apart. "Hey, what is it?"

Jade shook her head. "If anything happens to Rose…"

"Don't go there. Div needs her alive for now. He'll know you had been documenting what you found at the staging site. He can't afford to let those photos get into the hands of law enforcement."

Without thinking, Ethan covered her hand with his. He felt her tense and pulled away.

"Sorry," he murmured. "I'd forgotten."

Her shoulders sagged. "No, it's okay. It's me. I hate that about myself."

"Jade…" His heart broke for her. She'd lived in the shadow of what happened for so long. "None of this is on you. It isn't your fault what happened to you, and you certainly didn't deserve it."

She raised sad eyes his way. "Maybe, but I'm just so sick of living like this, Ethan. Never being able to make connections with others."

"I'm sorry," he murmured. The words felt so inadequate.

She forced a smile. "I don't mean to be so melodramatic." She brushed her hand over her eyes.

"You don't have to apologize. What Div did to you was unthinkable." Though she'd never told him the full extent of what that man had done to her, it didn't take much imagination to realize it went much deeper than a beating.

"I'm still alive. Arezo isn't," she said quietly. "Because of what happened to her and the attack, well, I was pretty messed up."

He remembered. She'd taken risks when she wasn't physically capable of doing them because, he believed, she didn't care if she lived or died.

"When I came home, Rose needed me, but I had nothing to give her or anyone. I traveled around the country while telling myself I was trying to find Div and bring him to justice for Arezo. In truth, I was running away from myself."

"Under normal circumstances, it's hard enough to survive returning home from war, but after what you've gone through, I can't even imagine."

Jade smiled sadly. "After what happened to our father, our lives were already pretty messed up. I hate that I let Rose down."

Ethan remembered Jade telling him one evening about her past. Her father had once been the sheriff in the Ruby Valley of Montana. According to Jade, he was an honest man who would never have committed the crimes he was accused of doing. But an old gas can was found near a house belonging to an Amish couple who'd died in a fire. That was his undoing. The can was confirmed to have belonged to Jade's father. The MO had tied her father to their deaths and several other arsons around the community. Since their deaths had occurred in the act of a felony, her father had been convicted for their deaths. The Amish family who'd lost their parents was Tanner Mast and his sister, Leora.

"You're here for Rose now," he said quietly. "She knows what you went through."

Her head jerked toward a faint sound before

she slowly relaxed. "We should probably keep moving."

She rose and dusted off her damp clothes. Ethan reluctantly did the same. He believed Jade when she'd told him her father wouldn't have done what he was charged with. Which meant the real killer was still out there somewhere.

As they continued walking, something grabbed Ethan's attention, and he stopped suddenly. "Hang on." There were three vehicles parked on the road. All were SUVs.

Jade's eyes grew wide as she faced him. "Rose may be in one."

All the more reason to be cautious. If Rose was being held inside and they got into a shootout, she could be injured or killed in the crossfire.

Ethan pointed to a group of trees nearby. He and Jade carefully advanced closer.

When they were almost even with the last vehicle in the lineup, Ethan noticed several men standing near the front of it. The hood was up. They were having engine trouble.

Ethan counted at least five standing by the open hood. There was no sign of Rose, but she could still be in one of the vehicles.

"I'll draw their attention to me. See if you can find Rose." He gestured to a vantage point where he'd be protected by trees. "When I'm in position and give the signal, go."

She nodded, and he eased toward the trees. Once Ethan was in place, he nodded. He and Jade moved nearer to the road.

Ethan did his best to see inside the vehicle closest to him but couldn't.

He stepped from the shadows. "Get your hands in the air," he yelled. All five jerked toward the sound of his voice. Ethan ducked behind the nearest tree. A breath later, the world around him exploded with gunfire.

Jade slipped around to the back of the broken-down SUV and peeked through the window. She confirmed it was empty. Rose wasn't in this one. Which left two more.

As she reached the front of the vehicle, one of the perps spotted her and whirled toward her, opening fire. Jade opened the SUV's door and used it as a barrier against the bullets coming her way. She was so worried Rose would get caught in the battle.

Dozens of shots tinged off the door while she waited for a break to fire back.

"Jade." The panic in Rose's voice coming from the next vehicle up ripped her heart to shreds. "Help me."

They had her sister.

"Get her into the lead vehicle. Let's get out of here!" someone yelled.

"Stop shooting, Ethan," Jade yelled. One stray shot and her sister could die. "I'm coming, Rose. Hang on."

The shooters responded by firing at the SUV Jade stood at and the location where Ethan was held up.

Car doors quickly opened and slammed shut on the lead vehicle. They were getting away with Rose.

Jade left her cover and ran after the two speeding vehicles.

She aimed for the lead one's tires but missed. Ethan raced from his cover and assisted. The shots sent sparks bouncing off the side of the vehicle.

"No!" Jade screamed and continued to chase them, but it was useless. The drivers pushed the SUVs to the limit to escape.

Ethan caught up with her.

She leaned her hands on her knees and tried not to give up. "I can't believe it. They have Rose, and I couldn't get to her." She was crying and couldn't stop herself.

"Hey." Ethan tugged her into his arms, and for once she didn't try to pull away. She held him close and cried like she hadn't in such a long time.

When she had no more tears left, she pulled away and wiped her eyes. "I'm sorry about that."

He brushed his thumb across her cheek. "Don't apologize. We'll get her back, Jade. I promise we will."

Jade desperately wanted to believe Ethan, but she'd had Rose and she'd let Div's people take her away. Had she blown her chance at saving Rose's life? Now that Div knew Jade was coming after him, would he eventually kill her sister?

Please, no.

"We should get going," she told him. "The other troops who were behind us will have heard the shooting and come to investigate."

"Yes, but first, let me take a look at the vehicle," Ethan said. "Maybe I can get it going quickly. Keep a watch for me."

Jade nodded and moved to the back of the SUV while Ethan worked on it.

She scanned the darkness. How far behind were those from the camp?

"I think I figured it out."

"Really?" Jade said in amazement and hurried to the front of the vehicle. "What's the problem?"

He pointed to the loose battery connection. "I'm really surprised those guys didn't see it." Ethan tightened the connection as best he could by hand and then closed the hood. "That should do it."

Which meant they would be able to go after Rose faster.

Jade climbed into the passenger seat while Ethan loaded the dogs into the back. He slammed the door shut and got behind the wheel. The keys were still dangling from the ignition. Ethan started the SUV with a sigh of relief.

"I'm going to try and maneuver down the road without using the headlights. If they are listening carefully, they might hear the SUV coming, but with the headlights it will be a dead giveaway. At least this will give us a fighting chance."

Jade opened the glove box. "It's empty." She frowned. The owner of the vehicle was probably trying to conceal their connection to it.

She searched through the center console and every single cubby inside, but there was nothing that gave any indication of who owned the vehicle.

Ethan guided the SUV carefully down the slick road. So far, there was no sign of the vehicle holding Rose, but its tracks were easy to follow.

As they continued down the road, her sister's frantic voice kept replaying through Jade's thoughts. Rose was scared and being held by dangerous criminals. Jade couldn't bear the thought of losing her.

Ethan's phone rang from inside his pocket. He shot Jade a look before he retrieved it.

"It's Sheriff Collins." He quickly answered it and put the call on speaker. "Boy, are we glad to hear from you."

The static on the phone was so loud Jade couldn't hear the sheriff's response.

"Say again, Walker." Ethan took the phone off speaker in the hopes of hearing his friend. "Hello…no." He pushed out a frustrated sigh. "I lost him." Ethan tried to call back. "There's no reception. I'm guessing we must have caught a pocket of service. Hopefully, we'll pick up the signal again. We'll find her." He glanced her way.

Ethan edged the SUV around a tight curve and then braked hard, throwing them both forward against their seat belts.

"What happened?" When he didn't answer, she focused on the road. A tree lay across it. "Can you go around it?" How had the SUV ahead of them gotten by the tree in the road? The answer became clear. "It was deliberately placed in the road to block anyone from coming this way."

The tension visible in Ethan's profile was alarming. "It's a trap."

No sooner had the words cleared Ethan's lips than the woods lit up with gunfire.

"Hold on." He reversed quickly. When the SUV was out of the range of the weapons, Ethan spun it around and headed back the way they'd traveled.

"Stop—we have to go back." Jade grabbed his arm. "They'll kill her."

"And they'll kill us if we go back there. We'll find another way to rescue Rose."

Jade looked over her shoulder in time to see multiple enemy troops emerge from the woods. "Duck!" she exclaimed. A heartbeat later, another round of shots had everything else flying out of her head except how they were possibly going to survive this attack.

TEN

One shot quickly took out the engine. Ethan lost all control of the SUV. It careened toward the steep drop-off beyond the road.

Jade screamed.

"We have to jump!" Ethan quickly unbuckled his seat belt and commanded the dogs to come up over the console so he could get them out of the vehicle.

"There's no other way, Jade. If we stay in the vehicle, we're going over the edge."

"You're right." She fumbled with the seat belt, her fingers trembling too much to free the latch.

"Here, let me." He slowed the SUV to a crawl and opened his door. "Go, dogs!" All three animals bailed from the SUV. Ethan tossed the backpack out and grabbed Jade around her waist. He hauled her over the center console and out of the SUV. He did his best to take the brunt of the landing, but both hit the ground hard. The breath evaporated from his body. Ethan struggled to catch it again.

He sat up, still holding Jade. The SUV hurtled over the side of the mountain, plowing a swath of earth until it reached the bottom and exploded into a fireball that rose into the sky.

"We've got to get out of sight now." Ethan rose on unsteady legs and lifted Jade up beside him. He motioned for the dogs to follow.

As he started down a less steep path, he kept his arm firmly around Jade's waist to support her. If they could reach the trees a little farther down the incline, they stood a chance of staying hidden, and hopefully their pursuers would think they'd gone down with the SUV.

At such a steep grade, it was hard to keep his feet beneath him. One false move and both he and Jade might end up with the SUV.

Over the noise of their labored breathing, another disturbing sound. Multiple footsteps.

"Can you run?" Ethan asked.

Jade nodded and pulled away so she could run on her own. With the dogs in the lead, she ran for the trees while he checked over his shoulder. Reaching the trees and getting out of sight before being spotted was critical.

At the edge of the trees, he stopped. Four flashlights scanned the area around where he stood, barely missing him.

He caught up with Jade. "Keep going." Would Div's militia send operatives down to search the wreckage? If that happened, it would be better for him and Jade to be as far away from the site as possible.

The path continued sharply downhill. After covering some space, Ethan stopped. "I don't think we're being followed."

Jade peered through the trees. "You're right."

"It's best not to use the road again. There might be snipers up on the road waiting to pick us off." He pointed to the path he and Jade would have to take. "It won't be easy, but it's the safest."

They started walking up the steep hill. Ethan kept close to Jade's side. The attack had happened so suddenly. It was frightening, the number of fighters in the woods.

Jade stopped. "Did you hear something?"

He listened carefully. A vehicle's engine fading. "They're leaving the area."

"But why not make certain we're dead?" Jade wondered aloud. "I don't get it."

Ethan could think of only one reason. Getting Rose out of the area. "I'm guessing Div wants Rose brought to him right away. Maybe he thinks he can bargain with her life to get us to back off and hand over whatever evidence you have against him."

Jade flinched as if he'd struck her. "Every

minute she's with those monsters she's in danger. I want her back, Ethan. I want her back now."

He wanted to reach out and gather her close, but he doubted she would welcome the gesture. "We'll get her back. I promise we will."

They started up the embankment. Snow made it harder to gain traction. Several times, Ethan slid backward and landed on his back. Jade had the same outcome.

After more than an hour of fighting the land, both reached the top of the embankment.

"Which way from here?" Jade asked.

He'd lost all sense of direction a long time ago. "To the left, I think."

After a break to catch their breaths, they followed the trail the dogs had left.

Ethan did his best to keep a close eye on their surroundings. By now, he believed the dogs had lost Rose's scent entirely and were simply moving forward.

"I'm so tired I can't even think straight, but I keep wondering about those armored vehicles. What part do they play in Div's plans?" Jade said as if trying to work out the confusion in her head.

"I don't know, but you can believe there's a reason—and one for why Div didn't have his goons keep coming after us. I'm guessing he's moving everyone to the place where they'll be the most useful in an attack."

The reminder of a possible impending attack gnawed at his insides. He and Jade were the only witnesses to the armored vehicles with the exception of a couple of Amish folks.

"I sure wish I understood any of this." Jade shook her head. "Who do you think Div is working with?"

He had been thinking about that himself. "Someone with a lot of power, who could grease wheels by bribing the necessary officials to get the weapons and tanks across the border."

Jade stopped walking and faced him. "Someone with a lot of money or perhaps a lot of political power."

While working special ops, Ethan had heard rumors from his intelligence friends about someone high up in the intelligence community being corrupt. He was known only as "Shadow" because no one had been able to ascertain his true identity. He told Jade about the speculation.

"Unbelievable. Whoever the person is, they no doubt have high-up security clearances. No one would question their actions."

Ethan agreed. "Want to see if we can put together a working theory?" She nodded. "So, Div, being a petty arms dealer, wanted something bigger for himself. To accomplish this feat, he'd either have to hook up with the money guy or perhaps he already knew him."

Jade frowned, and he added, "My guess is this person sought Div out. He needed someone who'd be willing to get their hands dirty."

"You mean like killing Arezo?" Jade asked.

"Exactly. They were probably working together back then."

"So, the mystery guy ordered Div to kill Arezo, only he hadn't planned on me knowing what Arezo had seen."

"Right. When you didn't let Arezo's disappearance go, the mystery guy ordered Div to handle you."

Jade visibly flinched, and he apologized. "Sorry."

She shook her head. "No, I understand. They couldn't just disappear me as a US soldier. When I returned stateside and kept digging…"

"Div got worried and had you followed. He's probably been watching you the entire time."

Jade nodded. "They found me in Idaho, the Pacific Northwest and Alaska despite my attempts at staying hidden."

"Div has probably known where you lived here in Montana all along. Much like the situation in Afghanistan, he couldn't take out a federal agent, but he sure could keep track of you in case you caused problems."

"Like following his shipment of weapons into the States."

Ethan nodded. "Div knew you weren't going to let it go. He kept you under surveillance in case you became a bigger problem than in Afghanistan." He faced her before saying, "And you did."

And because of her persistence, Rose might die.

"Hey, we know she's alive and close. We can't give up hope," Ethan said, drawing her attention back to him. She had to hold it together for Rose.

The dogs seemed to be moving with more of a purpose now. She held out hope against all possible odds that Molly, Nimshi and Trackr had found some usable trail. "I still can't get over the feeling that we're being tracked," Jade said.

"Yeah, me too." Ethan kept watch of their surroundings despite the darkness.

The vehicle had left the area a while ago, but what if there were still shooters out there waiting to capture them?

Walking through thick underbrush made it hard not to make a sound.

Jade spotted the road through the trees. "Over there."

"We can use it to navigate, but it's best if we stay clear of the road for safety purposes. Div's gang will be expecting us to use it to follow them."

As they walked, the road made a sharp left bend. Jade stopped walking. "Any idea where we are?" Ethan was more familiar with the countryside than she was.

"We're still heading for the mountain range. Stay close to me, though. I can't shake the feeling that we could be walking into another trap."

Keeping the road to their right, she and Ethan followed the dogs.

"I'm going to try Walker again." Ethan retrieved his phone and made the call without success.

What Jade wouldn't give for another flash of service. "Maybe the sheriff can use his earlier call to your phone to triangulate our location."

"Hopefully. But if not, then maybe Walker can track the dogs' collars." Ethan stopped suddenly. "I hear something."

Jade listened and her eyes widened. "That's running water." She rushed toward the sound. A makeshift bridge had been built to allow vehicles to cross safely. Down below, a river neared overflowing its banks. "Was this bridge here before?" She focused on Ethan and watched him shake his head.

"It wasn't. And the road was little more than a trail the last time I came this way. Someone's came along and built it up to allow for moving heavy equipment."

"Such as armored vehicles."

"At the very least." Ethan ran a hand across his eyes. "We'll have to use the bridge to cross the water. Be watchful."

A shiver sped up Jade's spine as she and Ethan moved to the edge of the road.

"Hang on a second." He removed the binoculars. "I can't see anyone." Yet the tension in his voice spoke of his concern. "Still, I don't like it." He looked into her eyes, and Jade was moved again by this strong and caring person. He'd been there for her after the attack in Afghanistan. He'd tried to help her after she'd returned, but Jade had been in such a bad place, she hadn't trusted anyone, not even herself.

"Thank you again, Ethan," she said without looking away. "You've been there for me when I needed you, and you've never let me go." She touched his arm. "It means a lot."

His eyes softened, and he stepped closer. "I'd do anything for you, Jade. I'm never going to let you go."

Her chest tightened as she wished for things she'd written out of her life because they were just too painful to think about.

He tentatively touched her cheek. She leaned into his touch, not wanting to back away.

"Jade…" Ethan pulled in a ragged breath as she searched his face. She'd give anything to know what he was thinking, but here in the middle of the wilderness with the threat of Div's army finding them was not the place for that conversation, and he must have realized it.

Ethan dropped his hand. "We'd better get across the bridge." His voice had a rough edge to it as his attention focused on the road beyond her shoulder. He stepped past her, leaving the coverage of the trees. All three dogs followed while sniffing the air. Even the animals seemed on edge.

Jade's breathing was anything but steady as she followed.

So far, there was no sign of anyone close.

She stepped onto the wooden bridge.

"I don't like this." The words slipped out as she and Ethan headed toward the opposite side of the river. She drew her weapon, and Ethan did the same. "Something feels off."

Ethan continued to survey their surroundings. "Agreed. Let's hurry."

Halfway across the bridge, a noise behind them had her whirling. "What was that?"

Before Ethan could answer, the crack of a weapon split the tension.

Ethan screamed in pain and grabbed his shoulder. The momentum of the shot propelled him several feet across the bridge and over the edge.

"Ethan!" Jade ran after him. She grabbed for

his hand, and he took her with him. They flew through the air and slammed into the frigid water. The cold knocked the breath from her. The force of the river ripped her jacket from her body. She went under briefly but fought her way up to the surface, though she'd lost the knit cap. Jade searched frantically for Ethan. He was floating down the river on the swift current.

"Ethan, hold on!" Jade stopped fighting against the momentum and let it sweep her after Ethan.

Over the raging water came the sound of the dogs barking frenziedly. The animals were no longer on the bridge but near the water's edge. Jade zeroed in on the bridge. Half a dozen armed combatants were there.

"Get under the water," she yelled above the noise and ducked below the surface as bullets peppered the water around her.

When she couldn't hold her breath any longer, Jade resurfaced. She didn't see Ethan.

"Ethan! Where are you?"

Near the edge of the river, a tree had fallen into the water. Ethan had managed to catch hold of a branch.

"Over here." He waved to her.

Jade fought the current while the shooting continued. Thankfully, they were out of range. She reached Ethan and grabbed hold of his hand. He tugged her over to the tree. Jade took hold of it and hung on. "We can't stay here. They'll come looking for us."

He glanced to the riverbank, where the dogs had appeared and were wading into the water.

"How bad are you hurt?" Jade asked when she noticed Ethan favoring his right shoulder.

"Not so bad. The bullet went straight through. Let's get out of here." He struggled and reached the bank before turning to help her out using his uninjured arm.

"Hang on. I've got to find Rose's jacket." She didn't know if it was possible to get a scent off it after being in the water, but she had to try and save it.

Jade frantically searched the river and spotted the red jacket caught up in some brush near the water's edge. She retrieved it and returned to Ethan. Having it in her possession was like holding a piece of Rose close.

Jade looked toward the bridge. "I don't see anyone." An uneasy feeling warned her that their attackers were still coming. Holding his shoulder, Ethan started through the underbrush at a fast clip. Jade raced behind him, stunned at the lengths Div and his militia were willing to go to silence Jade and Ethan…and keep their dangerous plan from being exposed.

ELEVEN

Ethan's shoulder throbbed mercilessly. Surveying the damage wasn't an option. Unfortunately, the bullet had struck his dominant arm, which meant using it would be difficult. If forced into a gunfight, he'd have to use his left hand.

Perspiration beaded on Ethan's forehead, yet he shivered from the cold. Both he and Jade were soaked from going into the river and in danger from the elements as well as the deadly assailants coming after them.

Lord, keep us hidden from these bad men, Ethan prayed frantically because nothing short of God's intervention was going to get them through this nightmare. A sense of calm settled around him almost immediately. It was always there when he communicated with the Lord. No matter what hardships Ethan faced, having that instant connection gave him peace of mind that he was never alone and there was a power much greater than him in control. While the shooters didn't appear to have found their trail yet, he had no doubt they would keep searching until they did because Div wouldn't accept failure.

The dogs quickly surpassed him. Ethan was grateful for the animals forging the way since the underbrush was so thick it was almost impossible to move through.

"Hold up a second." Jade caught up with him and touched his back. "I'm going to see if I can pinpoint their location."

"Jade, no, it's too dangerous."

"I'll be okay. Stay here and rest. We can't afford to run into Div's people by accident." She started away before he could stop her.

Ethan glanced around at his surroundings. The cold appeared to have intensified. Though the snowfall had lessened, it was still coming down, making traveling on foot almost impossible.

All three dogs stayed with Ethan as if sensing he was in trouble. Having the animals close was some comfort because he knew that should someone unwanted approach, they'd have his back. Still, every second Jade was away he was on edge. He had counted off the minutes she'd been gone. At least three.

Ethan peered through the denseness and saw nothing. He started back in the direction she'd headed when a noise nearby grabbed his attention, and he tucked in close to a tree. A second later, someone walked past his location. He followed their progression with his weapon trained. The second he caught sight of her hair, Ethan bent over in relief.

Jade jerked toward him. "Ethan—I could have shot you!"

"Sorry, I was worried about you." He and the dogs joined her and started walking. "Did you see them?"

"I did. They're down by the river searching the bank where we walked out. It's only a matter of time before they come after us. There's no way they can't see which way we've gone."

The last thing he wanted was another shootout. "Let's see if we can work our way back to the road while keeping lots of space between us and Div's troops."

Every step as they climbed the steep incline away from the river jarred his shoulder. Once they were on level ground, he and Jade circled back in the direction he believed the road to be.

"Here, let me carry the backpack." Jade eased the strap over his injured shoulder. Being free of its weight relieved some of the pain.

Jade retrieved the binoculars and searched the ground below. "I see them. They're on the move."

After they covered another quarter of a mile,

the road appeared ahead. Once more, they kept to the edge. The road made another sharp turn, and a valley stretched out below. He and Jade were heading straight for another mountain range.

"Did they use this road to move the armored vehicles?" Jade's question pierced through his thoughts.

"I guess it's possible, but it certainly wouldn't be easy."

"Ethan, if those vehicles are equipped with nuclear weapons, then this is far worse than anything Div has done in the past. He has to be stopped before he can finish whatever is in the works."

"And it's up to us to stop him." Ethan gathered his jacket closer around his body. Moving helped keep their body temperature up, but he was still worried about hypothermia.

The ground beneath their feet sloped gently downward as they headed for the valley below. All three dogs trotted out ahead of them.

Ethan sure hoped Walker was able to track their location and reach them before it was too late because he and Jade were grossly outmanned.

"I see something ahead." At his side, Jade stopped walking.

Ethan spotted several dark silhouettes in the distance. "Is that a ranch?"

She pulled out the binoculars once more and focused on the spot. "It is. It's dark, so I can't tell if anyone is still living there or not."

Fresh hope sprang to life inside him. "Let's find out."

The road wove down the valley, then suddenly veered off to the right and headed away from the property.

Molly, Nimshi and Trackr were heading for the house.

Jade frowned. "Do we follow the dogs and see if the occupants have a landline?"

Ethan didn't hesitate. "Absolutely. We need help."

They started down the valley to the ranch, where the dogs waited. It was the middle of the night, so he wouldn't expect there to be any lights on inside the house.

The house appeared typical of those found on any farm.

"They're probably sleeping," Jade whispered. "If it's even still occupied. I hate to wake the family up."

Ethan did as well. "Let's check around the place first. Just in case…"

Jade pointed to the barn. "Why don't we start there?"

The animals headed for the structure as if understanding Jade. Once she and Ethan reached it, Ethan opened the smaller side door. It made a yawning sound that grated along his frayed nerves.

Molly, Nimshi and Trackr rushed in first. Stepping inside, Ethan pointed to a buggy parked in the middle of the barn and realized the family who lived here were Amish. Stalls housed a couple of horses and a cow. "There won't be any way to call Walker."

"No, but let's try to wake the owners. Maybe we can warm up, and I can have a look at your shoulder before we continue." Jade was trying to stay positive. He should, too.

"You're right. It would be nice to dry our wet clothes and maybe stop shivering."

She smiled as they reached the porch. Ethan knocked several times. A faint light appeared through the curtains. A dying fire. Right now, that sounded like pure joy.

It took several more knocks before footsteps headed their way.

"I guess someone's awake," Jade whispered.

As they waited, Jade moved to the side of the house. "We've got trouble, Ethan."

He followed her and saw several flashlights moving their way.

"What do we do now?" she asked while keeping watch of the lights.

Trying to outrun the enemy wasn't an option.

He hoped the Amish family inside would trust them enough to give refuge.

The door opened. Jade shifted toward the light that spread out from the opened door. The dogs immediately took a defensive stance, ready to protect both Ethan and Jade.

"Who's out here?" a gruff baritone voice demanded.

She and Ethan returned to the entrance with the dogs close. A man who appeared to be in his fifties watched both with obvious suspicion.

"We're sorry to have woken you, but we need your help." Jade did her best to explain the danger they were facing.

After she'd finished, he stared at her as if she'd lost her mind.

"I know it sounds far-fetched, but if we can come inside until those following us pass. Please, they have my sister. We can't be captured. Rose's life is in danger."

Jade's heart sank when he continued to stare without saying a word. Had they wasted valuable time with Div's troops closing in?

"Sorry to have bothered you," she said with a frustrated sigh. "We'll be on our way."

She turned to leave when he spoke again. "*Komm* inside. You can wait until they're gone and warm up."

"What's going on, Amos?" A woman dressed in a prayer *kapp* and wearing a robe stood behind her husband.

Amos turned toward the woman and explained, mentioning Jade's sister.

"Oh, I'm so sorry. I'm Margaret. This is my *mann*, Amos. Please, *komm* in and bring the dogs. Everyone needs to warm up." Margaret noticed the blood on Ethan's coat. "You're hurt."

Amos stepped back and let Jade and Ethan inside. The dogs beat a path to the warmth of a woodstove. Amos stepped out onto the porch to make sure they were alone. Once satisfied, he shut the door and drove home the lock.

Jade and Ethan followed the dogs into the living room while Amos stirred the embers and added some logs to the fire. Soon it blazed warmly. Molly, Nimshi and Trackr settled in front of the fire, content to rest for the moment.

"I will get something to treat your injury," Margaret said before heading away.

"Do you mind if I check the back windows?" Jade asked, and Amos gave his consent.

She headed to the back of the house, still shrouded in darkness, and looked out. The flashlights were almost on the property.

Jade hurried back to the living room. "They're almost here. We have to get out of sight. Is there someplace we can hide?"

Ethan rose unsteadily. The dogs reacted to his movement and leapt to their feet. "Do you have a basement?"

"*Jah*, we do. This way." Amos headed for the kitchen. He indicated a door past the table.

Margaret glanced up as they entered the room. "What's happening?"

Amos told her about the enemy approaching.

Margaret grabbed the lantern from the table and handed it to Jade. "Take this. It's dark down there."

"Thank you." Jade pulled the door open. She started down the steps. The dogs passed her. Ethan was close enough for her to feel his breath against her neck. At the bottom step, she held the light up high. The space appeared to run the length of the house and was filled with shelves of canned goods. There was a workbench in the middle of the room that held tools. Perhaps Amos used the basement to do repairs when the weather turned ugly.

Molly sniffed around the workbench while Nimshi and Trackr explored the rest of the room.

"They'll stop to check the house," Ethan said.

Jade knew this in her heart. "I just hope they don't hurt Amos and Margaret." She listened intently. No sound came from above as the seconds ticked by. Someone pounded on the front door. Jade jumped in reaction.

The door above jerked open, and Jade grabbed Ethan's arm. Margaret stuck her head inside. "Oh, thank goodness," Jade murmured.

"They are here. Stay as quiet as you can." Margaret closed the door without waiting for an answer.

Molly kept close to Jade and Ethan, her hackles raised. She was on edge. Nimshi and Trackr watched the door where Margaret had been. Jade believed they all realized the impending danger.

Several voices could be heard at the front of the house. She caught Amos's but wasn't able to pick up what was said.

Jade's worried gaze latched onto Ethan. She still held on to his arm. Could feel the muscles beneath his jacket, strangely comforting. He placed his hand over hers while they waited.

More conversation drifted down their way. Jade caught something about footprints. Div's fighters had seen their footprints.

After what felt like a lifetime, the door closed.

"I sure hope they're leaving," Ethan whispered while keeping his attention on the door above.

Were Amos and Margaret okay? After some

time stretched on without any indication, Jade let Ethan go and hurried up the steps.

"No, Jade, wait." Ethan caught up with her and stopped her before she left the basement.

"They could be in trouble."

Before he answered, the door opened and Margaret appeared again. "They're gone."

Jade covered the rest of the stairs and stepped into the kitchen ahead of Ethan and the dogs. "What happened?"

"They were looking for you both," Amos answered as he came into the room. "I said you were not in the house—I guess that is mostly true since you were in the basement—but I'm not sure if they believed me. One mentioned seeing your footprints. I told them the footprints were mine and Margaret's. I said we'd gone to the barn earlier because one of the horses was spooked. Then we walked back to the house."

Would Div's troops believe the story?

"We'll give the enemy time to get out of the area, and then we'll leave," Ethan said. "I'm sorry we've caused you trouble."

Amos shook his head. "*Nay*, stay and warm up. Let Margaret fix you a meal and give those awful folks time to move on."

"Amos is right. You must eat something. Come and sit near the fire. You're bleeding. Let me bandage your shoulder."

"Thank you for your hospitality, but the sooner we're gone, the better it will be for you." Jade faced Ethan. "But you do need to clean your wound." She looked back at Margaret. "If you have some bandages and a washcloth."

"*Jah*, I have those. Come with me."

In the kitchen, Margaret brought out the items. She then grabbed a bowl and pumped water into it.

Jade helped Ethan out of his jacket then cut his sweater away enough to see the wound. Once she'd cleaned it, she was happy to see it wasn't as serious as it could have been. He gave her an appreciative smile that had her hands stilling on him. "It's not so bad," she said without looking at him. Her breath caught every time she was near him. She didn't understand this change in her. It was as if she'd been encased in ice all these years and now…

It was simply because she trusted Ethan more than anyone else other than Rose. He was kind and courageous. He'd tried to get her justice all those years ago after Arezo had disappeared. And then following what happened, he'd gone to bat for her with their commanding officers. Since they'd reconnected, they'd spent many hours talking about the difficulties of returning to civilian life. They had a lot in common.

Jade finished bandaging the wound. "I'm

going to slip outside and see where they're heading," she said in a less than steady voice.

She didn't wait for Ethan to answer. She quietly opened the door and stepped out into the night. Her hands shook, and it had nothing to do with those hunting for them.

Edging to the side of the house, she noticed the flashlights were moving past the farm. She just hoped there weren't others stationed nearby waiting for her and Ethan to make a move.

She stepped back inside.

"Everything okay?" Ethan asked.

Jade told him what she'd seen. "We should be safe to leave."

Ethan nodded and rose unsteadily to his feet. "Wait. You both need something dry to wear to fight the cold. Your clothes are soaked." Margaret removed two jackets from wooden pegs near the door. "Take these."

Ethan struggled into the jacket.

"Take some fry pies with you. You need something to eat." Margaret hurried to the kitchen and returned with a handful of things and two thermoses. "It's not much, but it will perhaps give you energy. And the coffee is hot." She had a bowl filled with water for the dogs. Each drank deep. Margaret gave the animals some leftover food.

Jade gently placed the fry pies along with

Rose's soaked jacket into the backpack before slipping into the coat Margaret offered. She hugged the Amish woman. "Thank you."

Margaret smiled sadly. "It will help you stay warm."

"Thank you both," Ethan said as they stepped out onto the porch with the three dogs.

"I hope you find your sister," Margaret told her earnestly. "I will be praying for you both and for Rose."

Jade squeezed her hand. She checked on the progress of the lights once more before returning her gaze to Ethan's.

"Ready?" she asked, and he nodded. They stepped from the porch and carefully moved past the barn while keeping a close eye on the activity on the road. Molly, Nimshi and Trackr took the lead, their noses to the ground as they intently searched for Rose's trail.

The brief reprieve in a warm house had taken away the chill from her body, but as the snow continued to fall and the temperatures dropped, it didn't take long to return.

Most of the trees had been cleared from the farm. Though it was dark, if anyone was watching, she and Ethan would be easy to pick up.

"I don't like being out here in the open like this." Ethan's words mirrored her thoughts.

"They're far enough ahead that it should be safe. Let's cross over to those trees."

Once they were in the woods, Jade relaxed a little. "Did you notice the road was pretty torn up? I'm guessing the armored vehicles came this way."

"No doubt. There's probably another camp up ahead of us. Hopefully, that's where they're taking Rose. We'll have to be careful." He looked her way.

She smiled into his handsome face. "How's your shoulder?"

He tentatively rolled it. "Much better. You did a good job."

"I wish we could have stayed for breakfast. I bet she's making eggs."

Ethan grinned. "Yeah. And probably bacon and toast."

"Oh, that sounds so good right now." She handed him one of the thermoses. "But we have coffee and fry pies."

Ethan unscrewed his thermos and took a sip while Jade handed him a fry pie. He took a bite. "This is good."

Jade claimed one for herself. She tried to remember the last time she'd eaten anything. Probably the sandwiches her boss had ordered for the team as they went over the upcoming court case against Zeke Bowman.

"How are you holding up?" Ethan asked. "You don't seem to be limping as much."

She realized she wasn't. And she'd almost forgotten about her side. "You're right. I guess walking for hours, falling into a river and getting into a shootout works wonders in helping to forget a bum ankle and a bullet wound."

He laughed. "Let's hope the rest of the journey is less adventurous."

She sure hoped so. She and Ethan had gone through enough danger to last a lifetime.

TWELVE

"Let's stop for a second," Ethan said because he couldn't shake the feeling that danger was close. The lights on the road were no longer visible, yet he couldn't relax. He grabbed the binoculars from the backpack on Jade's shoulders and scanned every inch of the space behind them. "Uh oh. We have trouble. There are several flashlights coming up. Not on the road—there in the woods." He handed the specs to Jade.

"Oh, Ethan, they're moving fast. At this rate, they'll catch us soon."

He searched the darkness for someplace to get out of sight. "Over there. There's lots of underbrush."

He commanded the dogs to follow. Ethan crouched low with Jade close. They'd barely gotten out of sight before a beam of light reached the spot where he and Jade had been standing.

Her eyes sought him. The look in hers made his chest grow tight. For a brief second, he forgot about the danger so close. Thoughts tumbled through his head that he hadn't considered in a long time. The rapid beat of his heart reminded him of how he'd felt when he'd first met Lee and had been swept off his feet by her smile.

Jade searched his face. "Are you okay?"

He looked away before he told her the dark fears of his heart. "Lee needed me to be here for her, but I was thousands of miles away fighting a war that wasn't winnable. I let her down. I don't want to let you down."

Jade clutched his shoulders. "You could never let me down, Ethan. And you didn't let Lee down, either."

But he had. In so many ways.

The crunch of numerous footsteps on frozen snow jerked him away from the sympathy in Jade's eyes.

Beams of light came close to their hiding spot. He fought not to react. It sounded as if there were a dozen or more soldiers moving through the woods. No one spoke. Ethan carefully placed his hand on Molly's head then Trackr and Nimshi in turn. The dogs waited for his next command. He held his hand out straight. Their sign to hold position.

Once again, Ethan was thankful for all the extensive training he and Fletcher had put Trackr and Nimshi through recently. They were smart and had caught onto the commands quickly.

It felt as if it took forever for the last of their pursuers to file past. Long after the footsteps faded, Ethan didn't dare move.

He could feel Jade's tenseness matching his. When the woods returned to a normal form of quiet, he slowly let her go.

"Now what?" she whispered.

He stood. "We give them time to get out of hearing, and then we follow. Hopefully, they're heading to meet up with the SUV that has Rose."

The desperation in her eyes didn't go unnoticed before she lowered them to the dogs, who were watching her and Ethan. "How many more are out here?"

"Far too many," he said with a weighty sigh that reached his soul.

"Whatever is going on, we don't have much time left to figure it out." The hard truth in that statement ground at his stomach.

He looked at her and wished he had answers to give. "We should be safe to start moving." Ethan gave the command to the dogs, who immediately started down the same path as Div's troops.

Beside him, Jade stopped suddenly. "I heard something."

He turned toward the direction she was looking. Before he could get the word out to run, four armed combatants emerged from the woods. They appeared as surprised as Ethan and Jade.

Jade dragged her weapon out and began firing. A keen markswoman, she struck her target, who dropped without a sound.

The remaining three whipped out their weapons. Ethan grabbed Jade's arm and tugged her into the protection of the trees.

"We're outnumbered. And the others will hear the noise and come to assist." Jade's urgent words got through the fog in his head.

Several shots landed all around. She was right. They had to extract themselves rapidly from the situation before the others showed up.

Ethan leaned forward just an inch. Immediately someone zeroed in on him. He jerked back. The shooters had them pinned down.

Jade pointed her weapon around the side of the tree and fired. Another cry confirmed a direct hit. Ethan took advantage and crept away from his protection enough to see the injured perp. He'd taken a direct hit in the arm and was screaming for help.

Ethan fired at the man trying to quiet the injured person. He grabbed his side and hit the ground.

The last one seemed to realize he was the only one still standing. He took off running in the direction he'd come. Not exactly the outcome they'd wanted, but time was critical.

"Let's get out of here." Ethan gave a short whistle to get the dogs' attention, and then he and Jade ran.

Soon, Trackr, Nimshi and Molly caught up. Ethan kept them all pushing through the wilderness. He wasn't sure which way they were heading, only that it was away from the clear and present danger they'd left behind.

Once they'd covered some distance, he slowed down while trying to control his labored breathing.

Jade struggled to catch her breath. "They seemed surprised to see us, but I'm wondering if perhaps it was just by how quickly they'd found us."

"Probably." He was worried they couldn't keep up this pace for much longer. But he'd promised Jade he'd help her find Rose. And he'd do everything in his power to make sure he kept that promise.

"We have to stop," Jade said. She had no idea which direction they were heading in. "I'm lost. Where's the road?" She glanced around. "We'll need to find our way back to it in order to get back on track."

Ethan did a complete turnaround. "Unless I'm way off, the road should be to our left."

Jade looked to where he pointed. "I think you're right." With the dogs sticking close, Jade tried to keep the noise to a minimum as they walked.

The last attack had been close. Her hands still shook. That she and Ethan were still alive was by the grace of God.

Please, protect her, Lord. I can't lose my sister.

Every time she thought about what Div might be putting Rose through, she wanted to scream or pound her fist against something. Jade knew what he was capable of doing better than anyone, and he would take pleasure in hurting Rose to get to Jade.

"Hey, we're going to find her." The direction of her thoughts must have registered on her face. "We know which way they're taking her. We keep pushing on until we have her."

Scalding tears stung her eyes. She wanted to believe him. "You really believe that?"

"I do," he said without hesitation. "You can, too."

The emotional exhaustion was the most debilitating. Keeping her thoughts straight and not going down frightening rabbit holes was hard. She'd gone over with a fine-tooth comb every fact, every detail she'd learned since she'd discovered Div was here, thinking she'd missed something important.

The thought that Div had been moving who knows what kind of weaponry into the country was more than alarming. At this point, it would be impossible to know what he had planned without capturing him, and right now, that seemed about as impossible as getting out of these woods alive. Getting Rose out of his clutches was one thing they could do.

Ethan stopped walking.

With her nerves on edge, she asked, "Did you hear something?"

He nodded. "Listen."

She heard it, too. "That's a vehicle." She searched his face. "It could be the one that has Rose."

She started toward the road when Ethan stopped her.

Jade swung toward him. Why was he hesitating?

"We have to be careful. After what just happened, the driver will be on alert. They'll expect us to come after them and be prepared."

He was right. If she and Ethan ended up killed, there would be no one to help Rose, or to let the Bureau know about what they suspected Div had planned.

She eased toward the sound while carefully watching where she placed each foot so as not to alert anyone who might be in the woods as well. Through the trees, Jade could make out a parked SUV near the edge of the road. It looked similar to the one carrying Rose. The passenger door had been opened. Jade and Ethan caught a glimpse inside. The vehicle was empty of all its occupants.

While they watched, someone entered her line of sight. He helped another guy into the vehicle. It was one of the men who had attacked them earlier. The injured man held his arm as he was helped into the passenger seat. A more severely injured one was carried by two others.

As soon as the injured were loaded in, the driver climbed inside and started down the road.

"I didn't see Rose in there." She turned to Ethan and saw he agreed.

"So, we're following the wrong SUV." If so, they'd lost hours that might cost Rose her life.

Ethan faced her. "Listen to me. Right now, that SUV is the only lead we have. We keep following it and the road and see where it leads. There's a very good chance we're going to find something that will help us locate Rose."

Ethan was right. They had nothing else. But after everything they'd gone through, Jade was still no closer to understanding what was happening than when she'd stepped into the woods and into the first of many attacks.

THIRTEEN

One thought kept tormenting him. Where had the virtual army near Amos and Margaret's place gone? He and Jade had made sure the troops had gone on ahead before they'd even left the farm. So, where were they?

The unknown made Ethan uneasy. Though Rose's trail had gone cold, the dogs had been working nonstop. Even though Trackr, Nimshi and Molly were accustomed to long stretches of hunting, they had to be exhausted. "How about we take a break and regroup? Let the dogs rest for a second."

Jade appeared to be barely holding it together. Both she and Ethan were injured, and they really hadn't had a second to catch their breaths. They would be no good to Rose if they dropped from exhaustion.

Jade's attention went to the dogs. "You're right. If we're exhausted, they are, too."

She placed the backpack on the ground and

brought out water. "We need something to give the dogs water in."

Ethan thought about the contents of the backpack. "The thermos lids. Those should work."

She retrieved the lids and filled both with water. Nimshi and Trackr drank deeply. She refilled one for Molly. "They are amazing, aren't they?" Ethan looked her way, and she pointed to the dogs.

"Yes, they are." Ethan had had the pleasure of working with Molly during several missions. When he was preparing to return home, he found out Molly was retiring from active duty, and he'd requested to adopt her. Lee loved the dog. After her death, Molly and Al were the only living beings who could relate to what he was going through. They'd grieved together. Eventually he'd found the strength to go back into the world.

"I remember you talking about Molly and the missions she worked with you," Jade told him. "I'm glad you adopted her."

"I am, too." He petted the dog's head. "She's been my best friend for a long time."

Jade studied him curiously.

"You enjoy working with Molly and the other dogs."

Ethan couldn't deny it. "They've taught me so much more than I could ever teach them."

The animals were loyal beyond belief and some of the hardest working warriors he'd ever encountered. They worked tirelessly to find their person under extreme conditions.

Jade smiled and handed him some water. "You never cease to amaze me."

He drank deeply without lowering his attention from her face. "You're pretty amazing yourself."

She dropped her gaze to the bottle in her hand. "I don't feel amazing. Just the opposite."

Ethan hated that she'd suffered so much at Div's hands.

"Look at me," he said softly. Her eyes slowly lifted to his. "You *are* amazing. The things you've gone through, and yet you are still standing strong. You saved my life. I wouldn't be here right now if it weren't for you."

"I have to take care of my lieutenant," she whispered softly.

"But I'm not your lieutenant anymore." The catch in his voice gave lots away.

Her eyes turned dark with emotion, and he couldn't take his eyes off her. Jade was so beautiful and so strong and his feelings for her were becoming clearer every minute he was with her.

He leaned closer. He wanted to kiss her more than he wanted anything. They were inches apart. Both breathing as if they'd run a marathon. Time stood still. Jade moved closer. She was coming to him.

As he waited for her, one of the dogs moved, and the spell evaporated.

Probably for the best. He couldn't let himself go where his emotions were leading him. Couldn't disappoint another woman the way he had Lee.

He stumbled to his feet. Jade stood as well.

"We should keep going." His voice came out gruff—not his intention.

She didn't say a word but retrieved the lids and shoved everything into the backpack before shouldering it. Soon, Jade fell into step beside him.

Up ahead, the dogs sought a trail. Ethan was grateful for the distraction of the dogs, which kept him from focusing on what had almost just happened. He wasn't ready to admit his feelings for Jade were anything more than caring for a friend. If he did, it would mean giving up this self-imposed state of martyrdom Ethan had banished his heart to because of Lee. If he let Jade in, he'd be betraying the love he vowed to have for Lee for the rest of his life. And if he let Jade in and couldn't save her...? His heart clenched at the thought.

"I see the taillights from the SUV." Jade's low voice interrupted his chaotic thoughts.

He squinted through the darkness and the trees.

"They sure aren't in any hurry to get their friends medical help," she said.

"I doubt that Div is too concerned with saving lives. They're all expendable. Let's keep following."

Jade remained still for a second longer before stepping forward.

Keeping enough distance between themselves and the taillights without losing track of them wasn't easy.

The SUV suddenly braked hard. He and Jade held up. After a few minutes, two men got out and carried someone to the back of the SUV. One man placed a jacket over the immobile person. The two returned to their seats and the vehicle started down the road again. "What was that about?" Jade asked while watching the taillights.

Ethan's jaw tightened. "I think one of those men we shot died."

"That's tragic," Jade said as they started walking again.

Ethan grunted his response while praying they would find Rose in time, but he had an ugly feeling time was running out.

The road took a sharp ninety-degree bend heading downhill.

Jade grabbed his arm. "I see multiple lights ahead." She quickly retrieved the binoculars. "It's some type of camp."

She handed Ethan the lenses, and he panned the area below. The camp appeared to be some type of temporary one. Several large tents had been erected around a cleared space. "Let's get a closer look."

The tension mounting between Ethan's shoulder blades warned of the danger they'd find below. If Rose was there, there would be no way to extract her without a shootout, and he and Jade weren't in the best shape.

As they neared the camp, he signaled for the dogs to remain close. The place was hopping with activity. Multiple vehicles were scattered around, and something was being loaded in the back of one.

"I can't tell what they're loading," Jade whispered. "But those look like the same types of containers Rose and I saw."

Ethan watched and tried to understand what he was seeing. "Do you recognize anyone?"

Jade searched the visible faces. "I don't think so." She turned to Ethan. "How do you want to play this?"

He thought for a moment. "Most of the activity seems to be focused on that large tent they're moving the containers from. We'll check the smaller tents first. Hopefully, she's in one of those."

His heart rate went wild as he and Jade moved to the closest tent. He ordered the two Saint Bernards to stay while he brought Molly along.

No light came from beneath the tent, so Jade lifted the bottom and slipped inside. Ethan glanced back at Trackr and Nimshi. Both dogs watched him. He confirmed the command once more and followed Jade.

The tent was dark, making it impossible to see anything. Once his eyes adjusted, Ethan noticed a couple of tables set up and what appeared to be boxes of cereal and other food stacked on them.

"This must be some kind of makeshift mess hall." Jade riffled through some of the boxes. "There's nothing useful here."

Molly sniffed the air, drawing Ethan's attention. "She's picking up on something."

"Maybe Rose was in the tent at one time," Jade concluded. "If so, they might have her stashed in one of the others."

"Possibly. Or she was taken somewhere different entirely." He saw her reaction and tried again. "We'd better check the rest of the tents. Let's keep looking." He held the edge of the tent for her and Molly. The next structure was some distance away. Ethan pointed to the trees. "Stay out of sight." He called Trackr and Nimshi over.

The three animals sniffed around, getting on the scent Molly had pinpointed.

Jade eased the bottom of the tent up and then quickly let it drop. She tugged Ethan away. "There's someone in there," she whispered.

"Were you spotted?"

Jade shook her head. "I don't think so, but it happened so quickly."

"Let's move a little farther away so we can see the front of the tent."

Once they were in place, Ethan asked Jade if she'd been able to make out anything inside.

"No, it was dark, and I only saw him because he had his phone out."

"He's probably alone." Ethan studied the tent. Should they search the other one or keep moving? Would they be wasting valuable time if Rose wasn't here? "We'll come back to this one."

Easing through the trees until he and Jade reached the next tent, Ethan peeked under the bottom. There was no sign of anyone. "It's empty. It could have been used to store some of the containers."

He kept his eyes on the dogs, who appeared to have lost their tracking scent. Even though they hadn't checked all the tents, the dogs' reaction pretty much confirmed what his gut was telling him. "She isn't here."

She released a breath. "You're right. At least, she's not in the tents. But she might be in one of the SUVs? After all, Molly appeared to pick up a scent earlier."

Ethan couldn't let her down. "Let's circle around behind the camp, and we'll see if the dogs pick up the scent again."

Jade slowly nodded. Moving through the heavy woods made it almost impossible not to make a sound.

Once even with the larger tent, Ethan gave the command for the dogs to search. It soon became clear they weren't picking up Rose's scent.

"I don't understand. I was so certain Molly was onto something."

"Search and rescue dogs usually have a high accuracy rate, but it's not unheard of for environmental factors to play a role," he told her. "And sometimes the dogs pick up scents that aren't connected." This was clearly not the news she wanted to hear.

Most of the SUVs were now moving from the camp. The last vehicle was loaded and idling, likely about to leave.

"Let's see if we can learn anything from what was left behind."

He gave the command for the dogs to stay and then moved as close as he dared to the front of the tent with Jade.

"They're not waiting for us," someone said with obvious irritation. Ethan peeked around the tent and noticed two men standing near the SUV. "I told everyone we need to stick together. We don't know if there are others out here looking for us."

Another said something Ethan didn't catch, but the first guy laughed. "You got that right. I don't know what he thinks he's going to do with the girl, but she's going to get us all in trouble. If he hadn't insisted we take her, there wouldn't be anyone up here looking for us now."

"Yeah. There's a lot at stake. Besides, he's not the one calling the shots."

Ethan's gaze slid to Jade's. They'd been right. Div wasn't the one in charge. Someone else with a lot of power was. Someone with far deadlier plans.

"Looks like we can leave now," the first one said.

A heartbeat later, two doors slammed shut, jarring Jade's frazzled nerves. Soon, the final vehicle was leaving the camp.

Jade eased toward the tent flap while watching the taillights pull out onto the road.

"Let's do a quick check around the rest of the camp and then follow," Ethan said.

"Copy that." Jade stepped inside the tent where

the containers had been. "It should be safe to use the flashlights, right?"

"I think so." Ethan clicked on his own and searched around the space. "There's imprints where the containers were."

Jade frowned and watched him kneel beside one. "What do you think it means?"

"I don't know. This camp hasn't been here long." He rose and faced her. "It was probably erected after the snow started. They placed the tent up and set the containers over the snow on the ground, and that's why we have the muddy imprints."

"So, they moved the containers here, and now they're moving them again?"

"Probably because of us. Div realizes we're looking for him and Rose, and from what that one guy said, he doesn't know if there are others who have knowledge of his operation. Though Div would probably have left the containers here for a bit, he doesn't have a choice but to get them out of the area."

"If that's the case, then the attack we believe will threaten national security might be postponed until the heat is off."

"Or they'll move up the schedule…"

Her eyes snapped to him.

If so, then the attack could happen at any time. Despite all their efforts, it might be too late to prevent it. Jade couldn't imagine the casualties that would be sustained. A further canvass of the camp yielded nothing of any value.

"Let's get out of here," Jade said in disgust. With the dogs in the lead, she and Ethan reached the road.

They'd been walking for some time when a sound caught Jade's attention and she swung toward it. A vehicle was heading down the road with its lights on bright.

"Get off the road." She had no doubt the light had picked them up.

With Ethan at her side, they raced through the woods, the dogs charging along with them.

On the road, the SUV screeched to a stop. Doors slammed shut. She heard multiple sets of footsteps enter the woods.

Jade's heart raced as she ran blindly through the darkness while the pain in her ankle as well as her side brought tears to her eyes.

Soon, the dogs overtook her and claimed the lead. Noises from behind made it seem a small army was giving pursuit.

Ethan glanced over his shoulder. "They're gaining. We'll never outrun them." He gave a short whistle, and all three animals returned to his side. "Through there." He grabbed Jade's hand and headed to the right.

The snowfall had picked up since they'd left the camp. Ethan continued to battle the thicket.

Jade's breathing was so heavy from the exertion of shoving branches aside that she was certain their location would be compromised.

"We can't keep fighting this. Over there." He shoved aside briars and knelt beside Jade and the dogs. She edged closer to him, needing his strength. Several combatants entered her line of sight. She clasped Ethan's arm and bit her bottom lip while praying desperately for God's protection.

Their pursuers stopped inches from their hiding place.

"Which way?" one asked.

"I don't know. I can't see anything. Use the flashlight."

"Are you kidding? We'll give our position away. Keep moving." The group eventually filed past.

"If we can make it back to the SUV, we can use it to get away," Jade whispered. "And maybe we can catch up and blend in with the other vehicles. Hopefully, they'll lead us to where Rose and the weapons are being held." Jade pulled in a breath and got to her feet. Before she and Ethan were able to leave their coverage, the group headed back.

"Get down." Ethan and Jade both crouched down once more as the fighters passed.

"He's not going to be happy," one could be heard saying.

"Not if we don't tell him," a far more assertive assailant insisted. "And I'm not going to tell him. Are you?"

The response was muffled. After their footsteps faded, the vehicle continued on.

"So much for my brilliant idea." Jade stood again.

"There's a good chance Div's fighters will be on the lookout for us even if they don't tell Div or whoever is calling the shots now."

Jade stared up at the sky as it steadily rained down snow. "We can't use the road." Even though it did make walking easier on her ankle.

"Yeah. I don't know if I have a whole lot of close calls left in me."

She smiled over at him. "Me neither. This is getting so out of hand."

He pulled out his cell phone. "I'm trying Walker again." A breath later, Ethan stopped short. "Hello? Walker, can you hear me?"

Ethan squeezed the phone hard as if he were trying to strangle it. "I lost him." He tried it again. "Straight to voice mail. Maybe if we move to a different location?"

They walked a bit and tried again. "Same

results." He typed a text message. "I think it went through. The bad news is my battery is almost dead."

Jade retrieved her phone. "Send him a message from mine and explain what's happened."

Ethan typed a short text and hit Send. He waited for a response. "Nothing."

"It may have gone through, but he may not be able to get a response back." She tried to stay hopeful. "Do you mind if we pray?"

FOURTEEN

Ethan checked both phones periodically for a response until his finally died. The prayer that he and Jade had shared had lifted his spirits. It reminded him that no matter what they faced, nothing surprised God.

"How about we take a short break?" Jade had started noticeably limping since their frantic jaunt through the woods.

"That sounds like pure bliss." She dropped the backpack and plopped down on the frozen ground.

Ethan laughed and did the same. He needed rest more than he cared about getting wet.

The dogs dropped down beside them. Ethan petted the animals. They'd been so diligent, but all had become weary.

Jade poured water for the animals before leaning back against the backpack. "All of this because of what?" She looked to Ethan for answers he couldn't give.

"Greed. Power. You name it. Why do terrorists do what they do?"

In the past, his team had been tasked with hunting down several terrorist cells operating in Afghanistan, and the reasons almost always boiled down to those. There were some who believed they were fighting a righteous war, but mostly they were after the power.

Ethan finished off the last of his water and watched as the dogs drank theirs.

"How's your shoulder holding up?" Jade asked when she noticed him rolling it to stretch out the tightness.

"Better than your ankle if the way you've been favoring it is any indication. Maybe I should take another look."

Jade shook her head. "I'm fine. You actually did a good job of wrapping it. I'll try not to put my full weight on it from here on out." She finished off her water. "There's only a couple more waters. Must mean we're almost finished with our mission."

He liked her positivity. "I sure hope you're right."

Jade smiled, and he didn't want to look away. His heart was softening up to her a little more with each look that gave him hope, and yet the guilt he'd carried with him for so long was right there in his head as well, reminding him of all the mistakes he'd made with Lee. He'd been consumed with the war and doing his part for freedom, and he hadn't even realized his wife was slowly slipping away.

Lee hadn't told him she was sick because she didn't want him to worry. When he came home, the change in her was dramatic, and his world collapsed. Less than a year later, he and Al were burying her.

A few months after, Al had passed away, and it was just Ethan. Alone with his war stories and his empty house.

"Are you okay?" Jade's question pulled him from the storm ravaging his heart.

He focused on Molly. "Yeah. I guess I was just…"

Jade leaned in close and touched his face, forcing him to look at her. The tenderness he saw there was for him alone. What he'd give to just let go of everything. Let the past be buried once and for all.

"She loved you, but she knew you were a soldier at heart," Jade said softly. "She knew what that entailed."

His mouth twisted bitterly. "But if I'd come home sooner, maybe I could have saved her."

Jade moved to his side and took him in her arms. "You couldn't. Your wife took care of herself. She went to her yearly exams. There was nothing you could have done to change it."

A sob broke free, and he held her close. He hadn't let himself seek out comfort. He was the one who always had to be strong. He'd shed his tears in private and brought Al home to live with him until his death.

"It's okay, Ethan. She knew you loved her."

He breathed out several shuddering breaths. "I know she did, but I still blame myself for her death," he admitted and saw her surprise.

"But why? She died from cancer. That wasn't your fault."

"It was. If I'd come home sooner, she might still be alive. I should have been there for her, and I wasn't."

"Oh, Ethan." The sympathy he saw in her was even harder to take. Jade believed he was a good person, but if he had been, wouldn't he have put his wife's wishes above work? Ethan slowly let Jade go but didn't move away. They were inches apart. He could see the exact moment when her compassion turned to something more. Something he felt as well. He leaned in and touched his lips to her forehead. Her eyelashes swept shut to hide her reaction, but he didn't need to see it. Something unexpected was happening between them even if neither wanted to admit it.

Was he ready to take that first step toward moving on without Lee? His heart urged him to say yes, but the past and his mistakes wouldn't let him go. He rose on unsteady legs. "We should keep going."

Ethan held out his hand. Jade slowly accepted it. He pulled her up beside him. She turned away and picked up the backpack.

"Here, let me carry that for a while. My shoulder feels much better."

She tossed him a look that said "You've got to be kidding me" and slipped it over her shoulders.

The dogs took up their hunt once more and trotted out ahead.

After what happened, it was safer to stay out of sight and keep the road to their left. So far, there hadn't been any other vehicles passing by.

"The first thing I'm going to do when Rose is safe is take a hot bath and build a fire. I'll probably sit in front of it for hours," Jade said, breaking the awkward silence.

He laughed. "That sounds pretty nice. Maybe have a cup of soup or coffee."

"Oh, I'll make some of my chili, and you and the dogs can come over. I can fix your furry friends a treat."

He stopped walking and faced her. "You have a date."

The smile on her face slipped a little at his choice of words. "Well, great then."

He placed a hand on her arm. "But first. We have to finish our mission."

She couldn't deny that she felt something. Had for quite some time if she were being honest with herself. Those quiet talks between her and Ethan up at her cabin where they'd shared the struggles of returning to civilian life, well, she'd found more peace with him than she had in years. But she was so closed off emotionally. How could she possibly hope to have a relationship with someone like Ethan? He deserved someone who could share their whole heart with him.

All three dogs had their noses to the ground, searching without success.

Where was Rose and where were they moving the weapons?

"Hang on a second," Ethan said, interrupting her musings. "Something's going on up ahead of us."

Jade stopped walking. Two of the SUVs were stopped in the middle of the road. Several armed gunmen stood around outside talking. A couple of voices sounded heated. What on earth was going on?

She and Ethan eased through the woods until they were parallel with the rear vehicle.

"What was your hurry?" one person said angrily while getting into another's face. "You hit us."

The offender being yelled at was just as angry. "I told you the road has patchy ice, and the breaks are bad."

"You know how sensitive those things are. You could have killed us all and then some."

Jade turned her head toward Ethan. *What are they talking about?* she mouthed.

He shook his head.

They continued listening as the men blew off their anger.

"Look, there's no harm done. I barely touched you. They're stable, so let's keep going. We have a deadline to make."

The person who had gotten in his face slowly agreed.

"You're right. Just keep your distance, okay?" He returned to the lead vehicle along with several others. The SUV took off. The rest got into the remaining vehicle and followed at a much slower pace.

"Please tell me they're not talking about some type of nuclear weapons," Jade murmured. "If not trained in the proper way to handle them, it could be bad." She raised her worst fears because she wanted Ethan to tell her it was impossible.

"It could be some type of suitcase, or as they're sometimes referred to, dirty bombs. If you had enough suitcase bombs, they'd be highly effective. Most have a three-to five-kiloton yield."

The warhead on suitcase bombs consisted of a tube with two pieces of uranium. When rammed together, they caused a blast. Still, there would have to be some type of firing unit and a way for the operator to ignite the bomb from a distance.

"I was thinking the same thing. I hope we're both wrong." Ethan whistled for the dogs to continue following.

"How is it possible they got their hands on nuclear warheads?"

Ethan shrugged. "Not so difficult these days. You can buy just about anything on the black market. It's possible."

"That's frightening." Especially in light of what they believed Div had planned. All the more reason to keep moving.

Jade examined the road for any sign of damage that would be caused by the tracks of the tanks. "There's no indication the armored vehicles came this way."

"They didn't," Ethan agreed. "So where did they go?"

Jade glanced around the dark countryside. "I haven't seen another road anywhere. Those vehicles are made to go off road. It would be nothing for the operators to do that, though traveling through these trees would be difficult."

"For now, let's not worry about the armored vehicles. We keep tracking the SUVs. I believe they'll lead us to where Rose is." Ethan looked over his shoulder. "Did you hear that?"

Jade halted. "There are others in the woods with us. It could be the rest of those goons who were pursuing us earlier near Amos and Margaret's." Before they had time to take cover, several armed combatants stepped from the trees nearby.

"Stop right there," one yelled as the rest ran toward him and Jade.

Jade dove toward the nearest tree. Ethan landed beside her as the first round of shots flew past where they'd been standing.

She scrambled to a sitting position. "How many?"

Ethan edged away from the tree. Another barrage of bullets had him ducking back. "I count three shooters."

"We'll have to take them out." There was no way they could outrun them. She just hoped the shooting wouldn't draw any unwanted attention.

Ethan waited until silence returned and shot

toward their assailants' location. "They're coming our way."

Their attackers probably figured they had Ethan and Jade pinned down.

"If you want to live, you'd better come out with your hands up now," one said.

Ethan held Jade's gaze. "I'm going to pretend to give myself up. As soon as you get a shot, take it."

She grabbed his arm. "What if they're bluffing and they shoot you?"

He skimmed her face. "Then get out of here. Do what you have to in order to stay alive. Find Rose." Without waiting for her response, Ethan called out, "I'm coming out. Hold your fire."

"Toss your weapon first."

Ethan hesitated for a second before reaching into his pocket and tossing one of the weapons he'd taken. "I'm tossing it out now." He threw the gun out, then tucked his own gun behind his back and out of sight. "I'm coming out with my hands up."

Ethan rose and put his hands in the air.

"Where's the woman?" the same one asked.

"She's dead. You shot her."

Ethan took a few steps toward the voice.

"You're lying. You're protecting her." To another, he said, "Go find her." The order was given. Soon footsteps came her way.

She'd have little time to take her pursuer out. Ethan would hopefully be able to reach his weapon and take out the one in charge. What about the third perp?

Jade pulled in a breath and held it. The footsteps came closer. As soon as he became visible, she struck. A single shot and he dropped on top of her. She struggled to get his weight off and help Ethan, but the guy had a good fifty pounds on her.

Multiple shots blasted on the other side of the tree while Jade fought like a wild animal to free herself. She finally wriggled loose and peeked around. Ethan was battling with the third assailant. The second lay on the ground.

Jade ran from her cover and rushed the two. As they were engaged in hand-to-hand combat, it was hard to distinguish between them. Jade waited until she had a clear vision of the bad guy and slammed the butt of her weapon against his temple. He stopped struggling and collapsed without a sound.

"That was close." Ethan breathed out. "Thank you."

He turned to Jade, and she noticed blood on his cheek. "You're hurt."

Ethan dabbed his finger against the spot. "It's just a graze. We need to secure these guys so they can't come after us again. I have some zip ties in the backpack. Is your guy still alive?"

"I don't know." Jade returned to the one she'd shot and felt for a pulse. There wasn't one.

She came back and knelt beside the person Ethan had shot. "He's still alive." Jade grabbed some bandages from the backpack and did her best to treat his injuries as he began to stir. "He's waking up."

Ethan finished restraining the unconscious guy then came over with the zip ties and secured the other assailant's hands and feet. With Jade's help, they leaned him up against a tree, removed the dead man's jacket and placed it around him. Jade found his phone and a second weapon. "We'll send help as soon as possible."

"You can't leave us here," the wounded perp raged.

"We'll send help. You'll be fine." Jade grabbed the backpack. She and Ethan stepped out of earshot while the conscious man screamed.

"I'm hesitant to gag those two, but if we don't, they'll alert anyone who's close, and we don't know how many more are out here looking for us."

She glanced back at the two. The second guy was now conscious and looking around wildly while jerking on his restraints.

"I don't think we have a choice." Jade ripped

off a piece of her jacket lining and silenced the two. She rose and shouldered the backpack.

Soon the muffled sounds of their attackers could no longer be heard.

"That was far too close," Ethan said. "If I hadn't turned sideways, I'd be dead by now."

She had no idea how close she'd come to losing him. "I'm so afraid there are others out here looking for us."

Ethan stopped and took her hand. "Probably, but we have to keep fighting. We've come this far. We can't let Div win."

She went into his arms and held him close. She just needed to hear his heartbeat against her ear—have that proof of life—and know they were both okay.

Ethan tentatively placed his arm around her and held her until she was ready to pull away.

She smiled at him and realized how comfortable she'd become with his touch. "I can't tell you how important you are to me, Ethan."

He stroked her cheek. "I feel the same way about you. I owe you my life, and so much more."

She took his hand in hers and squeezed it. "Let's finish this."

FIFTEEN

"Will you look at that," Jade exclaimed. "I think the dogs are on a scent."

Ethan's attention riveted to where the three trackers had their noses to the ground. As much as he wanted to believe they'd found Rose, it didn't make sense. Why would she be here?

Molly, Nimshi and Trackr crossed the road and ran into woods.

Her smile disappeared. "Why would they take her this way instead of transporting her by vehicle?"

He couldn't tell her his fears. "I don't like it, Jade. Keep your eyes open." He pulled out his handgun. With huge eyes, Jade did the same.

Keeping up with the dogs wasn't easy. The animals were focused to the point of shutting everything else out.

Ethan again tried to gain his bearings. With all the recent twists and turns, he'd become disoriented.

If his estimates were correct, the dogs were heading east. Away from the staging camp and the ranch where Div was last spotted. If they kept going, eventually they'd reach the North Dakota border.

His breathing had grown considerably more labored since the last shootout. Both he and Jade had been through more than either had prepared for. He wasn't sure they could withstand another attack.

Jade stopped suddenly. The dogs had disappeared. "Which way?"

He shook his head and focused on the ground and the paw prints.

Ethan headed through the thicket with Jade at his six.

The direction they were heading would lead them deeper into the woods and farther away from the road and the caravan. If they lost the vehicles, would he and Jade ever stand a chance of stopping Div and his coconspirator? Still, if there was even a remote chance Rose had been taken this way, he had to find out.

"Look, there's the dogs." Jade pointed to the animals.

Ethan spotted the three, and his heart sank. It was clear Nimshi and Trackr had lost the trail. "Molly has something." His stomach knotted as he headed toward the dog. Molly was trained in many forms of search and rescue…including detecting blood and cadavers.

Once he reached the spot Molly pointed to with her nose, Ethan knelt.

"Is that blood?" Jade asked.

He touched his finger to it and brought it up to where he could see. "It is." Ethan turned his head toward her. "We don't know it's Rose's." Yet something had happened here recently. Was it an animal or something far worse?

The fear on Jade's face made him want to reassure her everything would be okay, but he couldn't lie, and Molly had trained on the blood.

Ethan slowly rose.

"What if he's already killed her and this is all just some sick joke?" Her horrified expression told him she was spiraling.

He stepped closer. "Think about it, Jade. He still needs her alive."

She held his gaze. "But how soon before he decides it's too risky?"

Lord, help us find Rose alive.

Despite everything, he still had faith they'd find her before it was too late.

Ethan opened his arms, and she stepped into them. He held her close, and she didn't pull away. Holding her close like this was dangerous ground. He had feelings for Jade, but he needed to keep her alive. In the heat of battle, emotions had no place.

She pulled away, and he let her go. His arms dropped to his sides, and he felt deflated at the loss of her.

"I'm sorry," she murmured. She'd seen the rejection he couldn't hide.

"No, it's okay."

He wished things could be different. Wished she hadn't had to experience Div's brutality. Wished he could let his own ghosts go and give in to these feelings.

"I hate this," she said with a passion. "I just want to feel normal again. Being with you— working with you again." She looked over at him, and he wondered if it had been a slipup or if she'd meant something more. "It made me feel normal again." She shook her head, her expression forlorn. "Until I'm able to face Div again— put a name to the face in my nightmares and see that he is only a human after all—I will never have a chance to be normal again."

It broke his heart to see her so defeated.

She touched Ethan's face. "I want you to understand." She stepped closer. The look in her eyes begged him to understand, and he wanted to.

Before she could say what was in her heart, a virtual army appeared through the woods.

Ethan pushed her behind him. "Run." He barely got the word out before the enemy stormed their way. He grabbed Jade's arm and pushed her behind a tree and followed.

"Keep going," he told her. "I'll try and hold them off."

But Jade didn't budge. "I'm not leaving you behind, Ethan. No matter what happens, we stay together."

"How many?" she asked because she was terrified, but she knew the answer. Far more than she and Ethan could ever expect to fight off themselves.

"A bunch." He edged past the tree and started shooting, forcing some of the soldiers to take cover. "This is our only chance. Run." The dogs bounded ahead. Ethan reached for her hand, and together they ran through the intensely dark woods.

The group must have realized an escape was in progress and opened fire.

Jade jumped behind another group of trees, and Ethan slid in beside her. "We have to keep moving," she said. It was their only chance at escaping their attackers.

"Go, I'll be right behind you." He covered her with gunfire. Jade ran while keeping as low as she possibly could. In the gun flashes, she saw Ethan running her way.

"Hurry, please hurry," she whispered to herself.

Ethan reached her side and kept going. Both ran through the dense foliage. Soon, Jade could see the road up ahead. "We're almost there." But then what?

Another round of shots had both ducking low.

They were just a few short feet from the road when several SUVs barreled down it from both directions.

Jade stopped short. "What do we do?" She looked at Ethan and saw the same desperation on his face.

"This way." He clasped her arm and headed to the left. The dogs. Where were the dogs?

The last she'd seen them was when they were running the same way as her and Ethan.

Please let them be safe.

The woods weren't nearly as thick this way, making it easier to flee but also giving their pursuers a chance to zero in.

Jade struggled to keep going. Each breath burned her lungs. This was a nightmare that didn't seem to ever end.

Something charged toward her, and she bit back a scream. The dogs. She was grateful they were safe with the woods crawling with Div's troops.

"Up ahead!" one pursuer shouted. "I see the two. Bring the vehicles around." Their pursuers were trying to cut her and Ethan off. Several began shooting. Half a dozen bailed from SUVs to join in the pursuit.

"Keep left. It's our only chance." A beat later, the dogs realized the change and followed.

Multiple footsteps quickly drowned out the sound of Jade's frantic heartbeat. The woods were alive with armed opponents closing in.

"We can't outrun them forever. There are too many." Jade glanced over her shoulder. She and Ethan had fought so hard to find Rose—survived many attacks—was it all for nothing? Would they die here in the woods where no one would be the wiser?

Another look confirmed they were being hemmed in on all sides. "Ethan, they're all around us. What do we do?"

Ethan wore the same determined look she'd seen on his face whenever the situation seemed hopeless in Afghanistan. "We keep fighting. Mason and Fletcher will have reached Walker by now. He's looking for us. We just have to hold on."

She so wanted to believe him, but it was just two against a virtual army. Would help come in time? Rose's face appeared in her head. "I'll keep fighting. I won't give up."

A rapid succession of gunshots jarred her back to reality. Ethan pulled her behind some trees. He waited until the shooting stopped before running again, his hand still holding hers.

Soon, their assailants had picked up the location and opened fire, forcing Jade and Ethan to take cover.

Dozens of footsteps tramped through the woods toward her and Ethan's location.

Ethan grabbed the collars of the fiercely protective Molly, Nimshi and Trackr to keep the dogs from charging to their deaths. "Retreat," Ethan commanded. All three dogs disappeared through the woods.

Ethan turned his head to Jade and cupped her face. "They're going to capture us."

Jade shook her head. "No. There has to be something we can do."

He pulled her closer. "There isn't," he said gently. "If we keep resisting, we could be shot whether deliberately or by accident. If we surrender, we stand a chance. Div knows you have evidence showing what he's been up to here. He's vulnerable. Let's hope he's more worried about getting it than he is about eliminating us."

Not exactly the most assuring reason to give themselves up. Still, if there was even the slightest chance of being taken to where Rose was held, what choice did they have but to take it?

But giving up their freedom on a slim hope was terrifying.

"Don't shoot—we're giving up," Ethan called out.

The noise of footsteps halted. Silence followed.

"Toss your weapons out," a familiar voice responded. "All of them. We know who you are."

Ethan smoothed back Jade's hair from her face. He tucked one of the weapons into his boot. "Follow my lead."

Jade framed his face with her hands and kissed him tenderly. She didn't want to deny her feelings for him any longer. If this was going to be the end, then she was thankful her last minutes were spent with Ethan. For a second longer, she leaned her head against his before nodding. "Okay."

Ethan tossed out the weapons he'd taken from Div's fighters. Jade did the same.

"You'd better not be holding out on us," the same one yelled.

"That's all the weapons we have," Ethan answered.

"Then come out with your hands in the air."

Ethan's gentle gaze skimmed her face. "Let me go first. You stay behind me."

She loved him for trying to protect her. Loved? The thought took Jade by surprise. Did she love him? She wanted the chance to find out. To do so, they'd have to live through this.

"We're coming out." Ethan pulled in a breath and raised his hands before stepping from their cover.

Jade followed his lead. After her and Ethan took only a few steps, the troops converged.

"Search both," the person calling the shots yelled. "Thoroughly."

Jade was yanked away from Ethan. A person she didn't recognize did a thorough search, including checking her boots. He yanked her arms behind her back.

If they searched Ethan as thoroughly, his gun would be found.

As she watched in horror, Ethan was held by two while a third searched him.

Her heart sank when they found the gun. "What's this?" The weapon was removed from Ethan's boot.

The one calling the shots strode angrily toward Ethan and slapped him hard. "I thought I told you not to try anything. Take care of him."

Those holding Ethan tightened their grip while the third person slugged Ethan's midsection. He would have doubled over if he weren't restrained.

"Stop it! Leave him alone!" Jade yelled and tried to free herself.

The goon holding her smacked her hard. "Keep quiet."

Ethan was slugged again multiple times.

"Get them to the SUV." The leader growled out the order. "They've wasted enough of our time. And time is critical. We can't afford any more delays."

Ethan and Jade were forced at gunpoint to the vehicles.

"Well, what are you waiting for?" the leader demanded. "Get them inside."

Jade was yanked forward along with Ethan. The back hatch was opened, and Ethan was shoved inside first, followed by Jade.

Before she had time to think, the hatch slammed shut. Passenger doors opened. The vehicle began moving.

Ethan reached for her hand. Jade frantically turned her eyes his way. The look on his face held so much promise, but Jade was terrified they would die without knowing what happened to Rose. She couldn't give up anything else to Div. He'd taken too much from her already. She asked God to keep them all alive and give her the closure she so desperately needed as the SUV sped down the road toward an unknown situation that scared her to death.

SIXTEEN

Snippets of conversation drifted his way. Ethan listened intently. The person giving orders told another to dispose of any evidence of Rose and "the other one" once they reached their destination.

The other one? Fear coiled in Ethan's stomach. Had they taken someone else? If so, then why?

"Was it possible Rose went to the staging site with someone?" he whispered to Jade alone.

She shook her head. "No, at least she's never mentioned anyone before. Rose has been so focused on becoming a police officer that she doesn't really have a social life."

The person giving orders had a slight accent that could place him as from Afghanistan, but Ethan wasn't sure.

"Is that Div's voice?"

Jade's eyes widened as she listened. When the person eventually spoke again, Jade shook her head. "That's not him."

Ethan wasn't really surprised. Jade had always contended Div was American. While the SUV drove to their uncertain future, Ethan's mind ticked off every deadly outcome they might face once they reached their destination. He wondered about the dogs.

"Where do you think they're taking us?" Jade whispered in a shaky voice.

"My guess—wherever Div is hiding out." As he looked at her, he tried to remain strong for her. He wanted to memorize everything about her because he was terrified the future was slipping away.

Ethan's hold tightened on her hand. He tried to see through the limited window space provided through the hatch doors. All he saw was darkness. The skies were still dumping snow. It was still hours before daylight, and right now their only hope was riding on Walker being able to pick up the dogs' GPS.

With her eyes locked onto his, neither spoke as the SUV continued down the winding road. Ethan prayed for God's protection and for Rose to be kept safe until help could arrive.

His faith had been the only thing to sustain him through the dark time following Lee's death and then later Al's. It had grown stronger in his weakness, and he had to believe God was guiding their footsteps...even now.

A breath escaped and something shifted inside him. Righted itself. Some of the fear evaporated. He'd given their situation to God. Now it was time to trust Him to deliver.

"Hurry up," the leader said, breaking the tense silence. "He's waiting for us."

Ethan's full attention zeroed in on the conversation. Was it Div who was waiting for them to arrive or the person who was really in charge?

"I am hurrying. We're almost to the farmhouse now," a different voice said with impatience.

Ethan tensed as the vehicle slowed its speed. Jade inched closer.

"I'm worried," she said against his ear.

He was, too, but he was trusting God. "We'll be okay." He did his best to assure her of what he truly believed in his heart.

The SUV rolled to a stop. Doors opened and slammed shut. Footsteps headed to the back of the vehicle then the hatch opened.

"End of the road for you." One of their captors smiled down at them. He grabbed Jade first and forced her from the back. Ethan was dragged from the SUV. The one holding him shoved Ethan hard. "Get going."

Their captors were walking them toward a farmhouse where someone waited. As they drew closer, Ethan's blood ran cold. He recognized the man standing in the doorway immediately.

Miles Keller.

"Hello, Lieutenant," said Keller. Ethan was too shocked for words. At one time, Keller had been in his unit, long before Jade came on board. From the start, Ethan had had a bad feeling about Keller. Now he realized it had been justified. The man wore a satisfied smirk on his face when Ethan recognized him. "Long time, no see."

"You're behind this?" Ethan asked while still trying to understand what was happening.

Keller laughed as if Ethan had said something funny. "You should see your face right now. You weren't expecting to see me ever again, were you?" Keller's smile suddenly disappeared. "You always did have a poor opinion of me, *Lieutenant*." Keller emphasized the last word as if mocking Ethan.

"With good cause. I knew you were up to something illegal in Afghanistan."

The first time Keller had disappeared for a long period of time, Ethan had sent a search team out to look for him. He'd feared the worst and believed insurgents had kidnapped one of his own. And for a bit, that was what it had seemed like. Keller had been found and told the team he'd been taken hostage but managed to escape. Ethan hadn't bought the excuse because Keller didn't have a mark on him and seemed calm and collected. Ethan was pretty certain Keller had been up to no good. When it happened again, Keller claimed to have spotted his kidnappers and said he was trying to go after the enemy. Ethan reported Keller to his superiors, and that was when Keller's father, a senator, had stepped in and gotten his son transferred out of Ethan's unit.

Keller smiled again. "You always were the one who had to do everything by the book. You wouldn't give me another chance, so I had to call in my father for help."

"Your father got you out of my command before you could be punished for going AWOL. I'm guessing you didn't leave Afghanistan."

Keller's eyes gleamed like a child with a secret.

Ethan assumed Keller's going AWOL was more about him not being suited to following command or seeking to take some control back for himself. Keller had to be using his military missions as well as his contacts to both obtain and smuggle military weapons from the countries where he operated.

"So, you finally figured it out," Keller said. "Well, it doesn't matter now. You won't be around long enough to mess with my plans."

"Your plans? You're not the one calling the shots," said Jade.

Keller stopped smiling. His eyes flashed with anger as he turned to her. "Glad to see you again as well." He stepped to within inches of her, and Jade shrank back.

She was visibly shaken. She recognized Keller, too. Though she never knew Keller as a soldier, she knew him as the one who'd attacked her in Afghanistan.

Keller was Div, and he had Rose.

It took everything inside of her not to crumple to the ground in a terrified mess as the personification of her nightmares watched her carefully, knowing how much she still feared him. Though she'd never seen his face before, she'd recognize the voice. Jade would never forget the Midwestern inflection in his tone as he'd whispered in her ear while doing unspeakable things to her.

Another smug smile spread across Keller's face. "What—no words of welcoming for me after so long?" He lifted a strand of Jade's hair, and she jerked away. "Too bad."

She shoved the fear down deep. This man had her sister. "Where is she? Where's Rose?"

"You should have kept her out of it, Jade," Keller said softly. "What were you thinking letting your sweet innocent sister go out by herself?"

Ethan stepped closer to her side. She could feel him near her. Having him close gave her the strength to stand her ground and face down the one who had haunted her for far too long.

"Now, isn't this sweet. You think you can protect her, Lieutenant?" Keller was trying to bait Ethan.

When Ethan didn't respond, Keller grinned at Jade. "You want to know about your sister? Well, I'll tell you." He looked her in the eye. "She's probably dead by now, and you and Connors will be soon enough."

Waves of cold washed over her as her stomach contracted. She fought back tears. He'd taken Rose from her. "You killed my sister." She lunged for him.

Keller laughed and grabbed her hair, pulling her up close.

Ethan tried to fight his way free to help her, but two men restrained him, gripping him hard.

"You want to fight me?" Keller taunted close to her ear. "You won't win—ever! Did you think I didn't know what you were up to all these years?" His angry eyes bored into hers. "I know everything about you."

Keller released her and shoved Jade back against Ethan.

"Once you and the lieutenant are dead, there will be no one left to get in my way." Keller eyed them both with contempt. "It's too bad you two won't be around to see the plans I have in store for this country."

The words sent alarms crawling down Jade's spine. The first wave of attacks was only the beginning. Keller would keep coming until he was caught or he'd destroyed the country.

"You mean the country that you served and pledged your allegiance to? The country that your father still represents?" Ethan said with disgust.

Keller laughed, unfazed by Ethan's words. "My father is a joke. He uses his position as a senator to get what he wants. Why shouldn't I do the same? He's going to be surprised when he learns the truth. My father thinks he has power, but I'm about to show him what *real* power is when I implement my plan to bring this country to its knees. All those who think they make the decisions, like my father, are going to see how powerless they truly are."

"You're doing all this—are willing to destroy lives—to get back at your father? Gain power? You're not going to win this, Keller. We won't let you." Jade squared her shoulders as Keller came closer. She was face-to-face with the person behind her worst fears, the one who planned to kill both her and Ethan. She was done running away. He wouldn't scare her anymore.

Instead of being thrown off, Keller simply smiled. "My, my, aren't you the brave one. I guess maybe you didn't learn your lesson after all." He stopped a few inches away, and Jade lifted her chin. She wouldn't let him see how frightened she was on the inside.

Disappointment flashed briefly in Keller's eyes. He'd clearly expected her to cower in his presence. "You think you know the truth, don't you, Jade? All that research you and your meddling sister did, and you think you have it all figured out. Well, you don't." He shook his head. "Of course, I realized you were with Bowman as soon as I saw my guy escort you back to his vehicle, but I didn't warn Bowman because I wanted to see what you had planned. My men knew you were watching my activity at the border. Taking photos. I waited for the right time to take you down, and your sister delivered and made it possible."

Jade's heart sank. All this time, she'd thought she and Rose were hidden, but Div—Keller—had known she was here. Had known she was surveilling him because he was doing the same with her. He'd probably come to Montana on purpose to keep her close.

"Through it all, I knew I could count on one

thing. You wouldn't tell your colleagues at the FBI about me because you wanted to be the one to bring me down. You let pride win out, Jade. Not your brightest move." Jade couldn't deny she wanted revenge on Keller for what he'd done to Arezo and to her. But it had nothing to do with pride.

It was on the tip of her tongue to tell him there were police officers coming, but she didn't want to propel Keller into killing her and Ethan right there.

"So, who are you working with?" Jade kept talking even though she didn't believe he would tell her. She was stalling as long as she could while hoping Mason and Fletcher had accomplished their task and would bring the sheriff to their location. "Is it your father? He bailed you out in the past. Is he the real mastermind?"

Rage flashed on Keller's face before he struck her hard across her mouth. Her head swung sideways. Pain splintered from the contact point.

Ethan once more tried to free himself from his captors without success.

Jade tasted blood.

"My father has no idea what I am capable of doing, but he will soon enough," Keller said lowly. "And every negative thing he ever said to me, he's going to regret."

One thing became crystal clear. Keller had major daddy issues.

"My partner and I have plans that will shock the world. And when that happens, my father will see that he has no real power over me," Keller said with pride before apparently growing bored with their discussion.

Jade continued to pray unceasingly for Sheriff Collins to reach them in time. "So, you met someone who has a little power. Good for you. I guess you finally graduated from smuggling rifles and handguns off dead soldiers. You could never have done any of this on your own. You just aren't that bright."

Keller's face turned dark red while his eyes shot anger at her. He raised his hand to strike her again. Jade braced herself for the blow, but Keller lowered his hand and laughed.

"I know what you're doing," he said once he'd stopped laughing. "But it won't work. No one's coming to save you, Jade. You and our illustrious lieutenant have a date with death." Keller stepped away and motioned for several of his men to go with him.

He left the two restraining Ethan to keep watch. Both released Ethan and stepped in front of them with their weapons drawn.

Jade backed up so she was even with Ethan. "That's far enough. Don't try anything or you'll end up dead before your time," one of the guards said while keeping his weapon trained on her.

Jade turned her head toward Ethan. There were so many things she wanted to say to him. She cared about him. He'd made her feel again. She'd been locked into her nightmare for so long now. Living in fear. Terrified of any human contact. But Ethan's gentle care had begun to break down those walls that she'd built around herself and her heart.

He smiled at her. "We're not done for yet," he whispered so low that she almost didn't hear him.

Jade held on to those words and what she saw in Ethan's eyes because she didn't want this to be their end.

"I said keep quiet," the gunman moved closer, waving his weapon in their faces.

Both she and Ethan stepped back. Once satisfied he'd gotten his point across, he returned to his partner.

Jade focused on Keller, who appeared to be talking to someone with a satellite phone. She strained to hear what he was saying. Something about the time being moved up due to activity in the area. Keller glanced toward their location. When he spotted Jade watching him, he turned away and lowered his voice so she couldn't hear him.

The statement about the activity in the area made her wonder if the sheriff and his deputies were closing in.

Please, God...

Keller ended the call and spoke to several of those close by. After a brief conversation, many of the men headed toward the vehicles.

Keller moved to the two guarding her and Ethan, his gaze never leaving Jade's. "We need to go right away. Someone's coming. Take these two out to the woods and kill them."

Jade fought to keep from losing it. Help was on the way. She had to hang on.

Keller stepped to within a few inches of her once more, but the power he'd once had over Jade was no longer there. She'd been freed at last from his bonds by the prospect of death.

His eyes narrowed as he continued to watch her. "You should have kept your nose out of things, Jade. Back in Afghanistan and here. If you'd left things alone and not listened to Arezo, you and Rose would be living your life without a clue what was coming until it was too late."

The mention of Arezo almost broke her. "Tell me what you did to her." She had to know.

Keller smiled at her frantic reaction. "What do you think I do to those who cross me?"

"You killed her." She pressed him for the truth. She wanted him to admit what he'd done.

Keller turned to two of his soldiers without answering. "Take care of those two. Do it quickly and then catch up to us."

Jade glanced at Ethan and saw the truth. They had to figure out something quickly, or they were both dead.

"Are you a coward, Keller?" Jade yelled at his retreating back. "You want to destroy the country, well, why not tell the truth about what you did to one Afghan girl? You're going to kill us anyway. Who are we going to tell?"

Please have the sheriff hurry, Lord. We're running out of time.

Keller stopped midstride and slowly turned to her. "You really want to know what happened to Arezo, don't you? Why? What was she to you but an informant?"

Jade swallowed back the insult and tightened her back. "She was just a sweet young girl who wanted to help her country. She knew who you were, and she was trying to make you pay for what you were doing to her homeland."

"What I was doing?" he forced out. "I wasn't doing anything that dozens of others weren't doing. She should have kept what she saw to herself, and she would still be with her family."

Keller came close to admitting he'd killed

Arezo without actually saying the words. "You took her from her family."

He shook his head. "She did it to herself. Her family needed her, and she stuck her nose where it didn't belong. Arezo told you about it, and then you did the same thing. It got you into trouble, didn't it, Jade?" He said her name softly, and she winced. Keller was pleased with her reaction. "Ah, I see you remember our time together well." His gaze swept over her. "I'm glad to hear it. Just think how different your life might have been if you hadn't listened to Arezo. If you'd minded your own business and simply did your duty." He glanced at Ethan. "You and your lieutenant would be free to enjoy your lives. Instead, this is where it ends for you."

SEVENTEEN

Keller strode away after ordering their deaths as if he'd simply been directing some trash to be tossed away.

It sickened Ethan, the person Keller had become. The privileged lifestyle he'd led—his father's insulation—had left him with a sense of invincibility. Senator Keller loved his son yet refused to see that by bailing him out of every run-in with trouble, he wasn't allowing Keller to deal with the consequences of his actions.

"You heard the man," one of the armed guards nudged Ethan's side with his weapon. "Time to die."

It also sickened Ethan that anyone would follow someone like Keller. He couldn't imagine what type of propaganda Keller had used to recruit soldiers to follow him.

Ethan looked Jade's way and saw in her all the things he'd shut out of his life. Things he desperately wanted again. He couldn't lose her like this. He loved her and wanted to try to put his painful mistakes with Lee behind him once and for all. The way she looked at him made him believe Jade had feelings for him as well. With her help, he had a chance at happiness, and he wasn't about to let Keller and his goons take it away. Somehow, he'd find a way to overpower the two guards.

He caught Jade's attention and cut his eyes toward the two who were walking behind them. She quickly grasped his message and nodded.

"Keep going," one guard said, nudging Ethan with his weapon when his steps slowed.

Passing the farmhouse, their captors forced Ethan and Jade to keep walking. Out of the corner of his eyes, something grabbed Ethan's attention. Movement. Someone else was in the woods. He didn't believe it was Keller's militia.

Jade had heard it, too.

"That's far enough," the same person said.

"Wait, what was that?" The second guard stopped suddenly and looked around. Both had heard the noise.

"Go check it out," the mouthy one ordered.

"You go check it out." His counterpart wasn't happy to be bossed around. "I don't work for you."

"What's the matter? Are you a coward?"

"No, I'm not a coward. But you certainly are." With that dig, he headed toward the sound.

This was their only chance.

Before Ethan could make a move, Molly and her team of heroes charged from the woods and straight for the two captors.

Ethan leapt into action and went after the would-be leader. He shoulder-checked the guard, who went stumbling backward. Jade was engaged in a hand-to-hand battle with the perp near the woods. Before he could reach Jade to help, a gunshot ricocheted through the short space. Jade suddenly staggered backward.

"Jade!" Everything went into slow motion. "Hold on, I'm coming." But first he had to disable the shooter. He raced toward the man, who appeared as stunned as Jade did. Ethan raised his weapon and nailed him on the side of the head before he could react. He dropped to the ground as unconscious as his partner.

Jade stumbled and came close to losing her footing. He reached her in time. "I've got you." Ethan wrapped his arm around her waist. She'd been shot and was losing blood at a rapid rate. As much as he wanted to examine the wound and take care of her, Keller's goons would be coming to investigate the gunfire. Once they found the injured guards and spotted Jade's blood trail, it wouldn't take long to discern the direction he and Jade had fled.

She looked up at him with frightened eyes, and his heart was breaking. *Not like this...*

"Can you walk?"

She slowly shook her head. "I don't think so."

"Hold on to me. I've got you."

Ethan gently lifted her into his arms. She cried out when he came in contact with her injury.

"I'm sorry. I know it hurts." The nearby foothills were the only place he could think to take her.

He adjusted Jade's weight and ran. The dogs reappeared, flanking him on either side. He glanced over his shoulder. So far, nothing moved. Even if no one heard the shot, it wouldn't be long before the unconscious two woke up and alerted their team.

With the foothills in his sights, he kept running. The rocky terrain began to rise beneath his feet. "Only a little farther," he said before realizing Jade had lost consciousness.

Lord, please don't let her die. I can't lose her.

The prayer slipped through his head, and he tried not to fall apart. He couldn't give in to the heartache. He had to get her to safety. The snow had continued to fall, covering them both with a blanket of white.

Once he reached the foothills, Ethan searched around for someplace to take cover. He noticed a small opening in the rocks and ran for it. The opening would provide a small amount of safety and get them out of the weather. And hopefully give him time to examine Jade's wounds.

Div's goons had taken his backpack. All he had was what was on him. Thankfully, Ethan had confiscated both guards' weapons after the shooting, so he could hold off the enemy for a while.

He reached the space and gently laid Jade down. She groaned softly. Ethan dropped beside her, thankful for the small outcropping above that kept the weather from covering them with snow.

She was fading quickly, and his heart was breaking. He'd finally realized what God had been trying to tell him all these years. Lee's death wasn't his fault, and his life didn't end with hers. He had so much love still left to give, and he wanted to share it with Jade.

"Then help me," he turned his head toward heaven and begged God. "Hold on, Jade. Stay with me." His voice caught as he brushed her hair away from her face. "Everything is going to be okay."

He quickly ripped off pieces of his jacket lining and then removed his knit cap and placed it over the wound that had blazed a trail through her side close to the first gunshot graze. Ethan wrapped the strips of lining over the wound to secure it.

"Lord, please. I can't lose her." Ethan grabbed Jade's phone. There was no service, and he hung his head. "No." The word was ripped from way down deep.

Ethan rose and moved around a little before trying the phone again. The call went through to Walker.

"We've got you, brother."

Ethan doubled over with relief. Never had he been so thankful to hear Walker's voice. "You've been following the dogs' trackers."

"We have," Walker assured him. "We're on our way. From the GPS, it appears as if you're somewhere up against the mountains."

Ethan's worried gaze went to Jade. "That's right. Jade's been shot. She's going to need immediate medical attention."

"Roger that. We have Life Flight on the way as well. Are you safe?"

Safe wasn't something he'd felt since he'd awakened from a sound sleep to Jade's desperate call.

"For now. But not for long." Ethan explained as succinctly as he could what they'd gone through.

"Oh," Walker breathed the word out. "So, this Keller person was once one of your own?"

"Yes, he was. And his father is a senator."

"Brother, this is going to get real sticky. Sounds like we have a lot to catch up on, but first we have to get you and Jade out of there. We're close. Stay safe."

The call ended.

Safe. *Please, God.*

Ethan examined the makeshift bandage covering Jade's wound. So far, it seemed to be holding up.

Jade murmured something and opened her eyes. She glanced around. "Where are we?" When she tried to sit up, she flinched and reached for her side. "The last thing I remember is being shot."

"We're in the foothills past the farmhouse where we were brought." He filled her in on his conversation with Walker.

"Thank You, God." She smiled up at him. "I'm ready for this to be over." Her smile suddenly disappeared. "He killed Rose, Ethan. He killed my sister."

Ethan gathered her close. "I know. I'm so sorry."

Jade wiped her hand angrily over her eyes. "How's our position?"

Like him, Jade was a professional. She'd finish the mission one way or another.

"I'm not sure." Ethan couldn't see much, yet there was no missing the forms of the two he and Jade had taken out screaming at the tops of their lungs.

Jade struggled to stand.

"Stay where you are. You've lost a lot of blood."

She ignored him. "I'm okay." Ethan helped her over to the large rock that would provide them coverage.

"I hear vehicles," she said. "Someone's coming."

Ethan listened. She was right. What sounded like several vehicles were descending on the area. Keller's goons weren't taking any chances that they might escape.

A bunch of armed gunmen entered the clearing between the woods and the foothills, heading their way.

As Ethan and Jade prepared to defend their position in a last-ditch effort to hold on until the sheriff and his officers could rescue them, Ethan knew he would fight to the death to protect Jade. What he felt for her was every bit as real as what he'd experienced with Lee.

He wouldn't let Keller hurt her again.

"Hang on, okay? Just hang on and don't get shot again."

He held her close and prayed God would give them the chance at love they deserved.

Jade fought back tears as the combatants reached the rocky foothills and came within shooting range. She and Ethan were armed with only the two handguns he'd taken. Not much against an army.

"Use your shots sparingly," Ethan warned.

All three dogs were at Ethan's side, their hackles raised at the approaching threat.

She nodded. It wouldn't take long before their location was identified, and those armed soldiers would overrun this safe place.

Jade spotted one coming. She pulled in a breath and fired. The perp fell to the ground, but her shot's location wouldn't go unnoticed. Their location was compromised, yet there was no place to run. She and Ethan would stand their ground and pray help came soon.

"Watch out." Ethan grabbed Jade and tugged her behind him before shooting at another target. The advancing soldier grabbed his leg. Several shooters zeroed in on their hiding spot.

Ethan ducked low with Jade and waited out the storm of bullets landing all around.

When a tense silence followed, Ethan got to his knees and looked out. "The rest are almost here." He turned toward Jade. The hopeless look on his face scared her.

"Hey, we only have to hold them off until our help arrives." She didn't want him to give up. They'd fought too hard to give in now.

Ethan slowly smiled. "You're right. Walker is close."

Jade rose and peeked out at the sea of troops moving their way.

She fired into the crowd several times, forcing the troops to scatter and try to take cover.

How much longer could Ethan and Jade fight off so many?

"I hear the choppers," Ethan exclaimed and started laughing. "Jade, I hear the helicopters."

She glanced up at the skies. Several helicopters cleared the mountains behind their location.

"You're right." She hugged Ethan close. "We're saved."

"Look, Keller's guys are running for cover." Ethan pulled her along with him to watch the scene unfolding.

The helicopters found their targets and opened fire. Several of Keller's goons tried to defend.

Ethan aimed at several of the shooters, and all dove for cover.

"Those choppers are in danger." Jade was certain the shooters would regroup in the woods and attack again.

The choppers circled around looking for a safe place to land. Once they were on the ground, armed lawmen disembarked from the aircraft.

Ethan turned to her. "Stay here where it's safe. I'll send the EMTs."

She shook her head. "I'm going with you."

He didn't say it, but she understood he was worried. Still, she had to finish this. Had to find Rose's body and bring her home.

As they emerged from their coverage, another chopper cleared the mountains and landed close. It was an air ambulance.

Molly, Nimshi and Trackr were right at their heels.

A little way from their location, Walker and what appeared to be an army of police officers and FBI agents went after Keller's soldiers. One of the EMTs spotted Jade and Ethan and rushed to assist.

"She needs help immediately." Ethan helped Jade inside the chopper. He knelt beside her. "I'm going to assist Walker."

She grabbed his arm. "Stay with me, Ethan. You're hurt, too."

He smiled and brushed his fingers over her cheek. "I'm okay. Stay here and get looked after. I don't want anything else to happen to you."

She slowly let him go. Above all else, Ethan

was a hero whether he'd ever admit it or not. He was a true hero and had been to her since she'd first been assigned to his unit.

With a final lingering look, he stepped from the chopper and disappeared. *Protect him.*

"Ma'am, can you tell us what happened?" Dani, the female EMT, lifted the bottom of Jade's shirt and examined the injury.

Jade stifled a laugh as she told her how she'd been shot both times.

The woman's eyes met Jade's "How on earth are you even standing?"

Jade knew the answer. God…and Ethan.

She wouldn't be alive without either.

Gunshots resounded like a war zone beyond the safety of the chopper.

Jade tried to see outside, but the EMT gently pushed her back against the gurney. "They've got what's happening out there. Let us take care of you."

EIGHTEEN

Keeping low, Ethan reached the first chopper. He recognized the two Amish men who were easing out after the wealth of officers. His friends, Mason and Fletcher.

Both turned with their weapons drawn as he approached.

Mason realized it was him first and lowered his weapon. "Brother, I almost shot you."

Ethan reached the two and gave both heartfelt hugs. "Sorry about that. Boy, am I glad to see you and the cavalry."

Fletcher smiled. "Looks like you've been through a lot." His keen eyes skimmed over Ethan and his injuries. "Where's Jade?"

"She's getting treated by the EMTs."

"You should be, too," Fletcher told him when he spotted the blood caked on Ethan's clothes.

Ethan shook his head. "I'm still on my feet. I'm going to finish this for me and for Jade."

Mason nodded. "Walker is up ahead. His deputies, the state police and the FBI are here. Keller's troops won't get far."

Ethan sure hoped Mason's words proved true, but he wanted to catch Keller before he managed to get away so that he could find Rose's body for Jade.

By now, Keller would be desperate. And desperate people did deadly things.

"Stay," Ethan gave the command for the dogs to remain. The two younger ones grumbled but sat down while watchful of their surroundings.

As they reached the next chopper, the woods, a fierce gun battle was taking place. Flashes from gun barrels were everywhere.

He pulled in a breath and kept moving along with his two Amish friends. They reached the edge of the woods. The hair standing on his neck confirmed danger was close. He and Jade had been through so much already. He just wanted this to end and for Keller to face his crimes once and for all.

Rustling to his left had Ethan swinging in that direction. He spotted two of Walker's deputies and blew out a relieved breath.

"We have several of Keller's associates in custody already. Some are still held up in the woods over there," Deputy Megan Clark said.

A group of deputies headed into the battle.

"Where's Walker?" Ethan asked Deputy Ryan Sinclair. He'd had the honor of working with most of Walker's deputies while doing search and rescue missions.

Ryan nodded ahead.

Soon they caught up with Walker and Deputy Cole Underwood.

"I'm happy to see you," Walker told him. "How's Jade?"

Ethan believed she would be okay and said as much.

Walker nodded. "That's good to hear. Our officers are closing in on the remaining shooters."

They kept moving. Soon, they reached other law enforcement officers along with FBI agents who were cuffing many of Keller's goons.

"Get everyone to the choppers," Walker told his deputies, who began hauling prisoners to the waiting aircraft.

Ethan searched every prisoner. "Keller's not among them."

Several of the agents stopped, and Walker introduced Ethan to them and to the assistant director in charge.

"Keller's still out there," Walker told Assistant Director Davis.

"He's probably hiding. We'll check the farmhouse and see if we can find him. Where's my agent?"

Ethan told him about Jade. "She's going to be okay."

Davis nodded. "Good to hear. Let's find Keller and see if we can force him to talk. We need the name of the person he's working with, and we need it quickly. I called Keller's father. He's going to meet us here. Hopefully, he can make Keller see it's in his best interest to talk."

The woods thinned and Ethan spotted the farmhouse. As they approached, Ethan wondered how many were still with Keller. Or had Keller escaped using one of the SUVs?

Davis gave the order to search the house. Ethan and his Amish friends, along with Walker and his deputies, prepared to enter the front door. The agents got into position at both the front and back entrances. The command came to breach, and they rushed in.

The house was dark. Slowly, Ethan's eyes adjusted to the dim light inside. The team spread out and searched the ground floor without any sign of Keller.

Davis indicated his agents would take the second floor.

"There's a basement," Deputy Megan Clark said.

"We've got it." Walker led his team to the door. He slowly opened it and rushed down the steps. Before they reached the bottom, shots ricocheted off the walls.

"It's a walkout basement." Ethan spotted a figure standing near the door. It was Keller. "Drop the weapon, Keller," Ethan ordered. Keller shot again, and everyone ducked low. Keller made a run for it. "He's getting away." Ethan raced after and tackled Keller.

"Get off me!" he yelled as Ethan grabbed the weapon out of his hand.

Deputy Sinclair reached Ethan. He rolled off Keller and hauled him to his feet so that Deputy Sinclair could cuff him.

"Let me go. Do you know who I am? My father is a US senator."

Ethan forced Keller back inside the basement while a wealth of agents descended on the space.

"Everyone okay?" Davis asked.

"We're fine." Ethan handed Keller off to the deputy director.

"Get him back to the chopper," Davis said.

"You got it, sir," one of the Feds said. Two FBI agents escorted Keller out of the basement.

"Nice work, Ethan," Davis told him. "Care to sit in on the interview with Keller?"

He did, but first he had to check on Jade. Had to make sure she was okay because nothing else mattered but her.

* * *

Jade felt as if she'd been hit by a semitruck, but she was alive and moving, and she wanted to know where Ethan was.

"Ma'am, you really need to stay here and rest. You've been through a lot."

Jade turned to the EMTs who had helped her and smiled. "I'm okay. Believe me, I know how blessed I am to be alive, but I have to check on someone."

Both eventually nodded.

Jade stepped from the chopper and searched the sea of law enforcement officers. Molly, Nimshi and Trackr spotted her and came over.

"Good dogs." She leaned down and petted the dogs who had fought so hard beside her and Ethan.

Someone headed her way. Ethan.

She ran toward him, not caring about her injuries. Jade took him in her arms and held him close.

"Are you okay?" she asked, searching his face.

"You're asking me if I'm okay? You're the one who almost died."

She smiled through her tears. "I'm just so glad you're okay. Is Keller…?"

"In custody and about to be interrogated."

"Oh, thank goodness." She pulled away. "Now, it's your turn to be patched up."

"It can wait. I want to sit in on the interview with Keller."

She shook her head. "And so do I, but first you need medical attention."

Molly came up to Ethan and nudged his leg almost as if in agreement. He chuckled. "Are you two ganging up on me?"

"Yes, we are. Good girl, Molly." Jade grabbed his hand before he could protest and led him toward the medical chopper.

He chuckled at her insistence. "All right, but you're staying with me."

She smiled at him. "Absolutely. I wouldn't have it any other way."

Ethan called the dogs with them and they bounded out in front.

Jade never let go of his hand while the EMTs patched Ethan up.

"You're still bleeding," Dani said to her. "Let me have another look at your bandage." Still holding Ethan's hand, Jade waited while the EMT checked her bandage. "I'm going to change it out, but we need to get you and Mr. Connors to the hospital right away."

Jade shook her head. "Just change the bandage, and we'll come in once this is over."

The EMT's opinion was clear, but she seemed to realize it was pointless to argue. Jade needed to see this situation with Keller through and find out where Rose was.

Once Dani was finished, Jade and Ethan stepped outside.

"You really should go to the hospital," Ethan told her. "We can handle Keller."

She skimmed his handsome face. Realized she loved him and believed he felt the same way about her, but if she ever wanted the chance to have a future without Keller's presence in her head marring everything, she had to do something about it now. Only she had the power to end this suspended state she'd lived in for too long.

"I have to hear him tell me what he did to Rose and Arezo. I can't live without knowing."

He eventually nodded. "Okay. You should know Keller's father is coming here. There's a good chance he won't talk, and if his father's prior behavior is any indication, he will urge his son to request a lawyer if he hasn't already."

She nodded. "Still, I have to try."

Ethan told the dogs to stay.

"Ready?" he asked.

She was. No matter what, she was.

Once they reached the chopper where Keller was being held, Assistant Director Davis stepped out to speak with her and Ethan.

"Good to see you on your feet, Agent," Davis said.

Jade smiled. "Thank you. Is he talking yet?"

Her boss shook his head. "No. He asked for an attorney, and then his father arrived. He's in there with Keller now." Davis glanced back at the chopper. "Senator Keller asked to speak to his son alone."

Jade tried not to give in to the frustration swamping her emotions.

"If Senator Keller gets his son off with all the charges we have against him, then I no longer believe in the justice system," Jade muttered.

Ethan squeezed her hand. "He won't. It's going to work out."

She wanted to believe him, but her sister was dead, and her heart was breaking. So many had been hurt by Keller.

With the new day, the snow had stopped. Though it was still freezing out, at least they weren't getting covered with snow.

She was exhausted down to her soul.

"Do you think he lied about Rose being dead?" As much as she wanted to believe Keller's claim was just him toying with her, she couldn't let herself have false hope.

Ethan searched her face. "I don't know, Jade. I sure hope so."

A person she didn't immediately recognize

stepped from the chopper and searched for Assistant Director Davis. When he spotted him, he motioned the FBI agent over.

"That's Keller's father," Ethan told her. "I remember him bailing Keller out when he pulled his disappearing act under my command." Ethan's mouth thinned.

Both men stepped out of earshot and turned away. Jade couldn't hear what was being discussed, but the knot in her stomach wound tighter.

After what felt like forever, Senator Keller returned to the chopper, and Assistant Director Davis came over to where Jade and Ethan were.

"I've got good news."

Jade squeezed Ethan's hand tighter.

"Keller knows he's in a lot of trouble, and his father has convinced him to cooperate with us."

"You're kidding?" Jade couldn't believe it. "I want to be there, sir."

Davis inclined his head. "I figured as much." He glanced briefly at Ethan before returning his gaze to Jade. "I know what happened to you, Agent, and I wish that you had trusted us with the story. We could have helped."

Jade realized she'd made so many mistakes by not trusting those around her. By running when she should have relied on those who cared for her and stood her ground.

"I realize I messed up," she told him. "But I want to speak to Keller. I have to know what he did to my sister and to Arezo."

Davis slowly nodded. "I'm happy to let you ask those questions, but we do have a bit of a critical issue on our hands right now."

"Like what does Keller have planned and who is he working with?" she finished for him.

"Exactly."

As much as she needed answers about her sister and Arezo, the fate of the country was at stake.

NINETEEN

Ethan could feel the tension in Jade through their clasped hands as she once again faced down the monster from her past.

As they stepped into the chopper, the man seated there appeared a broken shell of the one he'd been earlier.

Gone was the smugly confident person who had taunted Jade with what he'd done to her sister and Arezo. Keller didn't look up as they came closer.

Senator Keller was in the seat beside his son. The senator's eyes flashed in surprise when he spotted Ethan before he returned his attention to the agent in charge.

"Are you ready to talk?" Davis addressed the question to the senator instead of his son.

"He's ready," the senator assured him.

"This will be recorded. And for the record, you've agreed to not be represented by counsel at this time."

Keller nodded and his father nudged him. "That's correct," he vocalized.

Davis nodded to the agent who would be recording the interview. Once he hit Record, Davis shifted his attention back to Keller. "Start from the beginning and don't leave anything out."

Keller stared at his hands as the story slowly unfolded about how he'd gotten involved with a terrorist organization led by someone with a whole lot of power both in Afghanistan and worldwide.

As he listened, Ethan quickly became convinced this was the same terrorist he and different branches of the military had been chasing for years. Shadow was believed to be behind numerous terrorist attacks around the world.

"I need a name," Davis interrupted Keller's tale. "The deal is off unless you give us the identity of Shadow."

"He'll kill me." Keller's frightened gaze latched onto Davis's.

"We can protect you, but I want a name."

Keller swallowed several times. "It's Jorad Yoder. He's the son of the US ambassador to Saudi Arabia."

Ethan didn't recognize the name. He glanced around at the faces of the agents as well as at Jade and could tell no one else did, either.

"How did you meet Yoder?" Davis asked.

The silence of the chopper was filled with anticipation.

"During my time in Afghanistan." Keller glanced at his father, who urged him on. "I was a soldier there for a time, until my lieutenant figured out I was up to something and reported me to his commander." Keller glanced briefly at Ethan. "I was smuggling weapons when I was under Ethan Connors's command—that's why I disappeared." He stopped for a breath.

"After I left Connors's unit, I stayed in Afghanistan for a time and continued smuggling weapons. My path eventually crossed with Yoder's. We became partners soon after. At first, I thought it was a good thing. I'd been supplying weapons to Yoder's organization for a while when Yoder asked me to come work for him. Before I knew it, I was in way too deep to get out alive."

Keller stopped speaking and grabbed the bottled water near his hand. He took a slug.

"What do you mean you were in too deep to get out alive?" Davis asked with narrowed eyes.

Keller's hands shook as he screwed the cap back on. "I mean he'll kill me. He's not the type of person you cross. Yoder was the one who ordered me to take Arezo and to hurt Jade Powell. His organization has sleeper cells operating all over the US and abroad."

The news was frightening.

"What does Yoder have planned?" Davis asked.

"He's planning a major attack very soon. He's waiting for me to arrive at a specific time. If I don't, he'll go ahead with the plan."

Jade glanced at Ethan. He could read her thoughts. Had they fought this hard to find out the truth only to be too late? "Yoder paid off border patrol officers to look the other way while we moved massive amounts of weapons into place here in Montana as a staging location. In addition to the guns and armored vehicles, Yoder purchased dozens of suitcase bombs."

Ethan and Jade had been right. Still, the news of how many bombs were out there was alarming.

Davis stepped closer. "Where can we find Yoder? I want to know where he's hiding, and I want to know now."

Keller grew frightened. All the more reason Yoder had to be found before he had the chance to fulfill his deadly plans.

"Now, Keller!" Davis smacked the seat in front of the man. He jumped and his gaze grabbed onto Davis's.

"He's at a ranch near the border. The same one where Zeke Bowman and I met. It's his place. Yoder's grandfather left the Amish community because he found it too restrictive but kept land there and passed it down to Yoder's dad, who became a diplomat. Now, the place belongs to Yoder."

"I need the exact location, and I want you to provide the locations of the sleeper cells here in the US and abroad." Davis handed him a piece of paper and a pen.

Keller picked up the pen, his hand shaking as he wrote down an address. He continued to scribble the locations of the sleeper cells in the US and around the world. It was alarming to learn there were so many globally. With Keller's cooperation, there would be numerous arrests soon.

Davis turned to Jade. "You have questions for him?"

Jade stepped forward while clutching Ethan's hand.

"You told me you killed my sister." Her voice cracked over those words. "I want to know where she is, and I want to know where you put Arezo. Her family deserves the truth. They deserve to be able to bury their daughter—I deserve to be able to bury my sister." Ethan put his arm around her shoulder.

Keller looked at her for the longest time, and Ethan wondered if this was the secret he would take with him to the grave.

"Answer the question, Keller," Ethan snapped. "You've done so much damage. You deserve the punishment you'll receive, but Rose and Arezo didn't."

"She's not dead," Keller whispered slowly. His eyes lifted to meet Jade's.

"I beg your pardon?" The shock on Jade's face matched Ethan's.

"I said, she's not dead. Your sister is still alive. I lied about her being dead earlier."

Jade stepped to within a few feet of Keller. "Where is she?"

Keller shrank back. "At the ranch with Yoder. She was alive when I saw her last."

But she was with Yoder, and according to Keller, Yoder was capable of horrible things.

They had to act quickly to get to Yoder before he got wind of what was happening and cleared out. Keller had said he was supposed to meet Yoder at a certain time. That meeting time had now come and gone. If Yoder managed to get away, they might never have the opportunity again to bring down one of the world's worst terrorists.

Keller would pay for what he'd done to Arezo and to Jade with federal imprisonment for treason.

Ethan touched her arm. She'd want to be part

of the team that went after Yoder. Bringing Rose home safely was key.

She turned to him. "Arezo." Ethan slowly nodded and stepped back.

"I want the truth. What did you do to Arezo? Her family has the right to know what happened to her. I'm not leaving without knowing."

Ethan wondered if Keller would give up his secrets and admit he'd killed the young Afghan woman. If he admitted to murder, the charges would be added to his sentence.

Surprisingly, he hung his head. "Yoder ordered me to kill her." It was quiet enough in the chopper to hear the breath Jade sucked in. She wanted to know the truth, but hearing it aloud was heartbreaking. "But I didn't," Keller added quickly. "I couldn't. I hurt her badly—like I did you—all at Yoder's request, but Arezo is still alive, though she doesn't remember anything. She's at the same location as Rose."

Jade seemed incapable of moving. "Are you saying Yoder ordered you to kill Arezo, and yet you didn't? You expect me to believe you've kept her alive all these years?"

Keller became angry. "I'm telling the truth. She's alive."

"What about Yoder? You said he's at the ranch. Wouldn't he have seen Arezo and realized you'd lied to him about killing her?"

Keller repeatedly shook his head. "He doesn't know where she is. He has no idea she's still alive."

Ethan wondered if this was all a lie created by Keller—was he trying to save himself in some way by pretending to be cooperative? Would they reach the ranch and discover Rose and Arezo were both dead? Keller might try to blame their deaths on Yoder to keep himself from extra sentencing.

"You'd better be telling the truth," Ethan warned. "If we find either dead, you're just as guilty as Yoder."

Keller's eyes flashed with anger. "I *am* telling you the truth. I'm helping you bring down Yoder and countless sleeper cells operating around the world. I've given you the woman who you thought was dead. I've done everything you asked of me."

Jade turned away with a disgusted look on her face. "I need some air." She rushed from the chopper. Davis followed her outside.

No matter what, Ethan wasn't about to let Keller get away with anything. "You think you're innocent in all of this?" The anger in those words brought Keller's attention to him. "You have armed who knows how many dangerous terrorists through the years, and you attacked a US soldier and almost killed her, not to mention…" He couldn't say what he suspected had happened aloud. It wasn't his place.

"You let a family believe their child was dead for years. And if you weren't caught now, you and Yoder would have fulfilled your plans to attack this country." Ethan's hands fisted at his sides. Somehow, he resisted the urge to grab Keller by the collar and drive home the truth. "You are anything but innocent, and you will pay for what you've done."

With those words, he stormed from the chopper and searched for Jade.

He found her talking with Davis while the dogs watched from close by. All three leapt to their feet at Ethan's approach. "Ethan," Davis acknowledged him quietly. "I was telling Jade that Keller won't be getting off with leniency. He'll never see the outside of a federal prison again."

Though it wouldn't do much to heal the hurt Keller had left in his wake, it was something. Ethan gave his dogs some attention before answering. "I'm glad to hear it."

"My agents are going to take Keller to Missoula, where he'll be questioned further. I'm assembling a team to go after Yoder and find both Rose and Arezo."

"I'm coming with you," Jade said before he'd finished.

Davis shook his head. "You've been shot twice. You're in no condition to engage in what will probably end up being a shootout with Yoder's men. He won't give up easily."

Jade squared her shoulders. "With all due respect, sir, this is my fight, and I want to be there when my sister and Arezo are found."

Davis blew out a breath and reluctantly gave permission. "All right, but you are not to take the lead. There are two additional helicopters arriving. We'll chopper everyone to the location where the rest of our agents are being sent to watch the ranch. From there, we'll go in using vehicles to keep the noise down. We don't want to alert Yoder to our approach." Davis pointed to the arriving choppers.

Ethan gathered the dogs and loaded them into one of the helicopters. Jade and the Shetler brothers followed him in. Sheriff Collins and his deputies got into the second chopper along with Davis and the other agents taking part in the operation.

Jade sat beside Ethan. "Do you think Keller's telling the truth? Are they both still alive?"

Ethan so wanted it to be true, but he had to caution her not to get her hopes up. "I'm not sure we can trust him. Keller is hoping to make himself look better by blaming everything on Yoder, but you can count on him being just as guilty as Yoder. He might not be as ruthless, but he's a bad person."

"I just hope this is the one time he's telling the truth."

Ethan reached for her hand. "Me too. Rose didn't deserve any of this and neither did Arezo. I can't imagine what she's been through all these years."

Jade shook her head. "Keller said she's hurt badly, and it's affected her memory. She might not remember Keller as a bad guy."

Ethan hadn't thought about the possibility that Arezo might think of Keller as a friend and be protective of him. "Let's hope she is able to remember what happened to her. Having her tell the Feds what Keller did to her will be another nail in his coffin." He glanced out at the new day dawning as the chopper's blades geared up. The machine was soon airborne, following the lead helicopter and Life Flight—a chilling reminder that where they were heading, there would be injuries if not casualties.

She's not dead...

Jade hadn't stopped praying it was true since Keller said those words.

Ethan squeezed her hand, drawing her attention back to him. "I'm okay," she tried to reassure him, but nothing was further from the truth. Physically, she was barely holding on. Emotionally, all she could think about was Rose and Arezo.

"How's your side?" He indicated the injury she'd suffered recently.

Jade forced a smile. "It hurts, but I'm still going on this mission."

He inclined his head. "I know, though I wish you wouldn't."

Jade touched her finger to his face. "I have to, Ethan. I want to be there when they find Rose. And if Keller was telling the truth, Arezo will need me. Hopefully, she will remember me." She blew out a troubled sigh. "I can't imagine what she's gone through." She leaned her head against his shoulder. The gesture felt as natural as drawing her next breath.

He touched his head to hers. "Will you do me a favor and at least stay close to me?"

She smiled at his concern. "Of course." Ethan was a special person. He made her want things that she'd shut out of her life—things she thought were impossible when her life appeared to be frozen in the past. But she felt something for him. She couldn't deny it. Was she ready to put the past and the nightmare that had happened to her behind her once and for all? Could she?

Jade glanced out the window as the chopper

ate up the countryside. There was no space in her head or her heart for anything until she knew for certain her sister was safe. If Arezo was indeed alive, she would have a long road ahead of her.

"Do you think he told the truth about Arezo?" Keller seemed to want to lay all the blame on Yoder, but she didn't believe for a second that was the case. Keller was the one who had hurt her. It was Keller who haunted her dreams. Yoder was certainly dangerous enough but, in her opinion, so was Keller. He had a chip on his shoulder against his dad and was determined to do whatever he could to bring him down.

"I want to hope so, but I don't trust Keller."

His answer hurt to hear, but it mirrored her own thoughts. She lifted her head and met his gaze. "I really don't understand why Keller would suddenly give us all the information and not try to save himself by talking to a lawyer."

Ethan nodded. "He's playing a game of sorts. We just have to figure out what his endgame is."

She had no doubt that Keller had something up his sleeve.

"We'll be landing soon," the pilot announced.

Jade sat up straighter and looked out the window as the chopper slowly descended, kicking up debris. Once they touched down, the pilot killed the engine. Ethan stood and helped Jade from the chopper.

Mason and Fletcher came over to where they were waiting for the final chopper to land.

"This has all been pretty shocking," Mason said with a firm set of his jaw. "My *bruder* and I were so afraid we wouldn't be able to get to you in time."

"Thank you for saving us," Jade told him. "Did you run into any of Keller's army along the way?"

She and Ethan had covered so many miles before Keller captured them.

"Not really. I think most were already farther up the mountain," Fletcher said. "Once we finally were able to reach Walker, it wasn't long before he picked us up and he was able to activate the tracking system for the dogs' collars. Of course, with the weather hindering getting a good read on the signal at times, we had to do a lot of guessing."

That she and Ethan were found at all was a gift from God.

Walker and his team came over. "Everyone needs to wear a vest. If Yoder is still at the ranch, you can be assured he's heavily guarded."

Walker handed each a Kevlar vest before he turned to the Shetlers. "I know you want to be part of this, but I can't authorize it." He hesitated in handing Ethan a vest, too. "You're a civilian, my friend."

Jade shook her head. "He's with me, Sheriff. I need him." She faced Ethan and held his gaze. She didn't want to look away because Ethan made her feel like she could be happy one day. With him.

"All right," Walker said. "But you two are staying here."

Mason held up his hands. "Understood. Be careful. This guy is a bad person, and if he feels as if he's trapped, you don't know what he will do."

The warning slipped down Jade's spine like a shiver. She shook hands with Fletcher and Mason. "We'll see you back here soon."

She and Ethan headed to one of the SUVs with the dogs. Mason was right. Yoder was a very dangerous person, and he had everything to lose. If he was trapped, he'd come out shooting in a last-ditch attempt to save his life.

Ethan loaded the dogs into the back, and he and Jade slipped into the backseat while Davis and their driver got in the front.

Jade couldn't help but wonder how Yoder managed to connect with all the sleeper cells around the world. There had to be some type of network. Somewhere on the dark web where they could go to communicate without being worried about retribution.

She told Ethan as much.

He frowned as he considered it. "You're right. Capturing Yoder is going to be the tip of the iceberg. There'll be others in power involved. I have no doubt."

The thought was alarming.

The lead SUV slowed to a stop behind a wealth of vehicles. The Bureau wasn't taking any chances on Yoder escaping.

Davis gathered his team around him. "Listen up. We don't know how many unsubs we'll find on the property, and we have at least two hostages reported on site, so be smart. Don't take any chances and don't let anyone leave. We go in on foot, and we go in silence." He showed the photo of Yoder to the team. "This guy is a wanted terrorist and believed to be responsible for countless attacks. We believe he may be in possession of nuclear materials, and if he's cornered, he'll do whatever is necessary to save himself."

TWENTY

Ethan could feel the familiar adrenaline rush that was always present whenever he prepared for a mission.

Jade glanced over at him as they neared the ranch. The fear on her face scared him. She and Ethan were behind a sea of FBI agents as well as the sheriff and his team and state police.

"Are you sure you're up to this?" he asked because she had lost all color in her face.

She stopped to catch her breath. "I'm sure. I just need a second."

He waited with her. "Promise me when this is over, you'll go to the hospital and get checked out."

She held her side and drew in several breaths. "I promise, but you have to do the same. We've both been through so much."

Ethan willingly agreed. He'd do whatever she wanted as long as he made sure she was okay.

"Let's keep going." Jade started walking

again. Ethan stayed close to her side. He wasn't about to let her out of his sight.

Soon, they caught up with the rest of the law enforcement agents.

The ranch was large and spread out. There was the main house and several outbuildings along with a barn.

"I see several standing guard." Davis surveyed the property below with binoculars. "No sign of Yoder or the two hostages." He gave the order for his team to spread out around the ranch. "We don't want Yoder escaping."

Ethan and Jade fell into step with Walker and his deputies.

The ranch backed up against a wilderness area. "If Yoder's bodyguards make it to those woods, it won't be easy to ferret them out," Ethan said.

Jade turned his way. "We can't let that happen."

They reached the fence along the property.

"If Yoder is watching for us, we'll lose the element of surprise. We move in quickly." Davis gave the order.

Keeping close to Walker's officers, Ethan slipped under the wooden fence and helped Jade through. All three dogs were sniffing the air. They knew danger was close and were on alert.

As they advanced on the house, Yoder's snipers spotted the movement and began shooting.

From what Ethan could determine, soldiers were stationed at all corners of the house. Probably around the property as well.

Jade and Ethan ducked behind an outbuilding with the dogs as Yoder's bodyguards pinned them down. Ethan edged toward the side of the building and fired while the rest of those with him did the same. Several of the shooters went down.

"The back of the house is cleared." Walker gave the order to advance.

"Stay behind me," Ethan reiterated, and Jade didn't argue. She fell in behind him as they reached the back of the house.

Gunfire resounded all around the property. Davis's agents were engaging Yoder's people. Ethan edged around the side of the house with Jade close. Several of Yoder's guards fired on the agents. Jade and Ethan hurried to assist. When a brief reprieve sounded, Ethan said, "Let's keep going." His pulse pounded in his chest as they advanced to the front of the house.

A fierce gun battle was taking place there.

With Walker's officers closing in on one side and Ethan and Jade on the other, many realized they were surrounded. One by one, they lowered their weapons. While the agents cuffed the prisoners, Ethan and Jade headed for the Amish farmhouse. Yoder was still at large. Until he was captured, the place was still unsecured.

Ethan ordered the dogs to wait outside while he and Jade entered the house along with several agents. Ethan indicated he and Jade would clear the rear of the house while the agents took the front.

Room by room, the house was secured. Yoder was nowhere inside.

"We'll check the basement," one of the agents said.

"The woods," Jade exclaimed. "If he reached the woods, he could be hiding there, or worse."

Ethan agreed—it made sense. Yoder would want to get as far away from the house as possible because he'd know they'd search it first.

Several agents went along. Ethan grabbed Walker and a couple of his deputies.

As the group entered the woods, Ethan was on edge. Yoder was obviously smart. He would try to hide out rather than engage the officers.

Ethan gave the command for the dogs to search, hoping they might be able to locate Yoder. Molly, Trackr and Nimshi started through the underbrush. The dogs kept their noses to the ground. Before long, Ethan recognized Molly's bark. "She has something." He ran toward the barking.

Yoder crouched behind a tree. "Call your dogs off," he exclaimed while keeping a close eye on the three animals.

"Get your hands in the air," Jade ordered. "It's over, Yoder."

Ethan called the dogs back to him. Now that the immediate threat had passed, Yoder brandished a gun at Jade. Ethan's pulse went ballistic. He wouldn't lose her to this terrorist. Not when they were so close to having this nightmare over.

"Drop it, Yoder." Ethan advanced closer, shielding Jade with his body.

Yoder glared at Ethan and the other officers pressing in. He seemed to realize it was pointless to fight.

"Okay, I'm lowering it." He slowly dropped the weapon.

Several agents rushed forward and grabbed the gun and cuffed the terrorist known as Shadow.

"On your feet," one of the agents ordered and hauled Yoder up.

"Where is my sister?" Jade demanded. "Where is she?"

Yoder simply glared at her. "I don't know what you're talking about."

Jade stopped inches from his face. "You do. Rose Powell. Your little minion Keller told us she was being held here by you."

Yoder gave an ugly smile. "She was, but she's not anymore."

Jade jerked back as if he'd struck her.

Ethan stepped forward and pulled her away. "He's lying, trying to throw you off. Let the agents take care of Yoder. Let's get the dogs back on Rose's scent."

She slowly nodded and dragged her attention from Yoder. "You're right. I know you are."

Ethan headed back to the house with Jade. They'd done a thorough search inside. If Rose wasn't being held in one of the outbuildings, then where was she?

After everything they'd been through, would there be enough of Rose's scent left on her jacket for the dogs to pick up? Jade shared her concerns with Ethan.

"Let's try. The dogs have amazing noses. It's been estimated they are between ten to a hundred thousand times more acute than humans'."

Once the dogs had the scent, Ethan gave the order to seek.

The ranch was buzzing with activity. Davis was bringing Yoder toward one of the SUVs that had converged on the ranch. Yoder was quickly loaded inside to be transported to Missoula.

Soon, the dogs appeared to be on scent. Molly—in the lead—darted toward one of the smaller outbuildings on the property and some distance from the house.

"They have something."

Jade prayed all the way to the building.

A lock had been placed on the door. To keep predators out or humans from seeing what was inside?

"Stand back and watch your eyes," Ethan told her. "I'm going to break the lock." Jade moved away and called the dogs.

Taking out the handgun that he'd recovered from one of Keller's cronies, Ethan slammed the butt of the gun against the lock. It took several tries before the lock broke free and Ethan was able to remove it.

He glanced at Jade before opening the door. The dogs ran in ahead of him and into the building.

Jade was shaking all over as she entered the single room. Ethan found the switch and flipped on the overhead light, sending the darkness fleeing. The room had feed stored inside. She didn't see the dogs.

"Over there." Ethan had spotted Molly's tail and hurried past a stack of feed. "She's here."

Jade raced after him. Her hand flew up to cover her mouth when she spotted her sister bound and gagged in the corner. Rose's frantic gaze found hers. Jade dropped to the floor beside her sister. "Rose, oh, Rose." With Ethan's help, they removed Rose's restraints. Jade untied the gag and hugged her sister tight. "Are you hurt?"

Rose shook her head, her eyes huge and frightened. "I'm okay."

"Did he…" She couldn't bring herself to say the words aloud.

"No, he didn't. I'm fine, Jade, really. Just scared."

Jade helped her sister to her feet. "Can you walk?"

"I think so. Get me out of here."

"We'll need to get you checked out by the EMTs." Jade kept her arm around her sister as the three headed from the outbuilding along with the dogs.

"I'm fine. Just a little shook up is all." Rose got a good look at her sister and gasped. "What happened to you?"

"We had a run-in with Keller and his gang, but they're all in custody now along with Yoder. They can't hurt you again." Jade remembered what Keller said about Arezo being alive still. "Did you see another woman being held here?"

Rose frowned. "No, why?"

Jade told her what Keller had said about Arezo.

"Wait, this is the Afghan woman who supposedly died? So, she's actually alive?"

"According to Keller." Jade had hoped he was telling the truth. After all, what would it benefit Keller to say Arezo was alive if it weren't true?

Davis came their way. "You must be Rose." He held out his hand. "I'm Assistant Director Davis. If you're feeling up to it, I'd like to ask you a few questions."

Rose looked to her sister before nodding. "Of course."

"Do you want me to stay with you?" Her sister had been through so much. If she wanted Jade at her side, then that was where she'd be.

"No, go—find that girl. Find Arezo."

Jade smiled and hugged Rose once more. "I will." And she would. No matter what had happened to the young woman, she would find her.

Davis walked Rose over to one of the SUVs and helped her inside.

Jade glanced around the property. "There are so many buildings. Where do we start?"

Walker and his deputies joined in the search. And Mason and Fletcher were there as well. Walker must have given them permission following Yoder's capture.

"She could be in any of the buildings here on the property," Ethan said. "If we split up, we'll find her sooner."

"Copy that." Walker directed two of his deputies to search the buildings on the far side of the property while he and Mason and Fletcher took the ones east of the property.

If Arezo was anywhere on the ranch, they'd find her.

"Let's start with the shed next to the barn." Ethan pointed to it.

A large barn sat a little away from the house. Nearby was a smaller shed. Unlike the outbuilding where Rose was held, the door to the shed wasn't locked.

Would Keller have put Arezo in an unsecured location where she could possibly escape, or where anyone could walk in and find her?

"She's not going to be here." Jade pointed to the lack of a lock. At this point, they couldn't afford to rule anything out. She opened the door. A single bulb had a pull string attached, and Ethan reached for it and turned the light on. The room had a couple of shelves along two of the walls, where saddles had been placed.

"You're right—she's not here. Let's try the barn."

The barn was an enormous space lined with stalls that housed several horses.

A set of stairs led up to an enclosed space above. "There's an apartment upstairs. That wasn't part of the original Amish barn, I'm guessing. Yoder must have added it later." Ethan started up the steps. Jade fell into step behind him. On the landing, a door had been locked from the outside. Jade's pulse picked up. "This has to be it."

Ethan once again forced the lock free. Inside, a small living room and kitchen appeared neat and tidy. A hallway led to two doors.

Following Ethan's lead, she saw that the first door led to a bathroom. The second was locked.

Tension coiled through her body as Ethan felt above the doorframe for a key and found one. When he slipped the key into the lock and opened it, the room was dark. Jade found the light switch and flipped it. A woman crouched behind the bed, her dark eyes filled with terror. Jade recognized her right away.

They'd found Arezo.

TWENTY-ONE

"Arezo." Jade started for her, but the woman shrank away. She didn't recognize Jade at all.

"Arezo, it's Jade Powell. We met in Afghanistan while I was in the military." Jade didn't get too close. She didn't want to frighten Arezo any more than she was already.

The young woman stared with huge eyes before finally speaking. "I'm sorry. I don't remember you, and my name isn't Arezo."

Jade glanced at Ethan, who was no doubt a witness to the heartbreaking pain on her face. He squeezed her shoulder. Arezo's memory of what happened to her at Keller's hands had been wiped clean.

"We need to get you to the hospital," Ethan told the scared young woman.

Arezo repeatedly shook her head. "No, I don't want to go. He'll be mad."

"Keller is going to jail for a very long time.

He won't hurt you again, Arezo," Jade assured her. "I promise."

"I told you, my name isn't Arezo. It's Sarah."

Keller had changed her name to keep her identity hidden.

"I know he told you your name is Sarah, but that's not true," Jade said gently. "You are Arezo Karzai, and you are from Afghanistan. You have family there who miss you greatly."

Tears filled Arezo's eyes. "How can that be? I don't remember anything before I woke up in a bed, and he told me I was his sister."

Keller had lied to her and made her believe she was his family. The guilt he must have felt at what he'd done to her had kept him from killing her. He'd had to change her name to make the story believable.

"I'm going to call for medical assistance to take her to the hospital," Ethan told Jade and stepped out into the living room to call Walker.

"We found her," he could be heard saying. "She's in the barn, and she needs to get to the hospital right away. Arezo's been injured in the past, and it's affected her memories. She doesn't remember anything."

The paramedics arrived before Walker.

"She's in here, but she's pretty scared," Jade explained. "Maybe we can have just one of you go inside?"

Dani, one of the paramedics from the helicopter, volunteered. As soon as she stepped into the room, Arezo reacted with fear.

"No, please." Arezo began to back away.

"She's here to help you," Jade told her. "I'm going to be right here with you through it all."

Jade glanced Ethan's way and smiled before Ethan closed the door and stepped outside to wait for Walker.

While it might be a blessing in disguise that Arezo couldn't remember the horrific things Keller had done to her, Jade prayed one day she'd be able to recall the family who loved her and had never stopped looking for her.

"We're going to take you to the hospital now," Dani told Arezo. "I promise you are going to be in good hands, and your friend here is coming with you."

Arezo's frightened eyes searched Jade's face.

"I'm not going to leave you, but you need medical help to recover your memories."

Arezo's eyes filled with tears.

"Let us help you."

Arezo slowly nodded.

Jade smiled in relief. "Let's get you out of here and into the chopper."

Jade and Dani helped Arezo outside, where Walker and Ethan waited nearby.

Jade introduced Arezo to the two men. "There

have been a lot of people looking for you," she said and smiled.

"It's nice to meet you, Arezo," said Ethan. "I've heard a lot about you through the years. Jade never stopped looking for you."

"Really?" Arezo turned her head to Jade. "Thank you. I confess I don't understand any of this, but I've always believed what my broth... what *he* told me wasn't the truth."

"It will come back," Jade assured her. "It might take some time, but it will return."

And she believed that with all her heart.

Jade faced Ethan. "I'm going to ride with her."

He nodded. "I'll have Walker bring me in."

"And you're going to get checked out while you're there," Walker said from beside him.

Jade smiled at the sheriff. "Good idea." She touched her side. "Maybe I'll do the same."

Once inside, the pilot didn't waste time getting airborne.

"If you'd like, I can check your bandages," Dani told her while her partner kept a close eye on Arezo. "It's still a good idea to have one of the ER doctors do a thorough examination, though."

"Thank you."

Jade bit her bottom lip when Dani examined the dressing. "There's still a little bleeding, but the bullet went straight through, so barring any infection, you should make a full recovery," the EMT said.

Jade kept a careful eye on Arezo as they landed on the hospital's helipad. Arezo was rushed inside. Dani gave Arezo's history to the doctor who would be treating her.

"You can trust him, Arezo," Jade assured her when the woman shrank back.

"Looks like you could use treatment as well." The doctor motioned one of his colleagues over to assist Jade.

Once she was treated and given extra bandages for the wound as well as a prescription for antibiotics, she waited for the doctor to finish with Arezo.

He stepped from the exam room to speak with Jade. "I understand she was taken hostage from Afghanistan?"

"That's correct." Jade told him Arezo's story.

With a grim expression, the doctor told her Arezo had suffered a traumatic brain injury that had not been treated. "This is no doubt responsible for her memory loss. I'd like to keep her here for a while. I've asked the hospital's neurotrauma specialist to consult. He will no doubt order an MRI and possibly a CT scan. Once we have a clear idea of the damage, we will know better how to move forward with Arezo's treatment. We're hopeful that in time those memories will return."

It was possible Arezo would one day remember what Keller had put her through. And when that happened, Jade would share her story and hopefully help her friend to see that none of this was her fault.

"Thank you, Doctor. Is she awake?"

"She is not. We gave her something to help her sleep. You can sit with her if you wish." The doctor smiled and stepped away.

Jade went into her room and sat down beside the sleeping woman. No matter what Arezo faced, Jade would be there with her every step of the way until she could safely reunite with her family.

Ethan found her and came into the room along with Walker.

"How's she doing?" Ethan asked as he stood beside her.

Jade told him what the doctor had said. "She's got a long road ahead."

"But she's a fighter. She'll get through it. And we have some good news."

Jade listened while he told her about the plans the FBI had found at the ranch detailing the elaborate multiple-state attack Yoder and Keller had mapped out. "Thanks to the information, the FBI was able to get to the locations and stop the attacks."

"Was it true? Did Yoder have suitcase bombs?"

"He did," Walker told her. "But they've been confiscated, and we're confident the threat has been contained. Agents around the world are arresting the sleeper cells, though it could take a while to pick them all up. But I believe we've broken up Shadow's terrorist organization for good."

"That's so wonderful to hear." Jade remembered the thumb drive with her surveillance of Keller and told Walker about it. "I hid it in my Jeep. There's a secret compartment in the door of the passenger side."

Walker nodded. "I'll have one of my deputies retrieve it and get it to Davis." He turned to Ethan. "I'll leave you two alone."

Walker stepped from the room before she could respond.

Ethan pulled up a chair beside Jade and reached for her hand.

For Arezo, everything was just beginning, but for Jade, the closure she'd so longed for was close.

As she looked at the man who made her feel again—the one she truly loved—Jade realized how much she'd need Ethan's love and support to be able to finally lay to rest what happened to her and move beyond the fears. Ethan had always been a man of honor in her mind. She'd need him now more than ever.

"What's on your mind?" he said in that husky voice that made her smile.

She faced him and found the courage to tell him about the rape. Speaking the truth aloud was freeing to some extent because it felt as if some of the power of what had happened to her was being taken away, yet she was terrified of how he would react. She couldn't lose him. Ethan was too important to her.

"That's the real reason why it was always so hard to let anyone close to me," she said after she'd finished. "I don't want to live paralyzed any longer."

"I know—that is, I guessed as much, but I'm glad you told me." The smile that spread across his face had her spirits soaring. "I'll always be there for you no matter what you need—you just have to tell me, and I'll make it happen. But there's one thing you need to know. You saved me, too."

The sincerity in his eyes made her not want to look away. She'd begun to heal even before she'd faced down Keller, and it was all due to Ethan's gentle care.

"I know what it's like to have a tragic event keep you from moving forward in life." He searched her face. "I loved Lee, but she's gone, and she wouldn't want me to mourn over her forever. I want a chance at the happiness I see with you, Jade. I'm ready to love again. With you."

Tears filled her eyes. "I'm ready, too." She leaned in and cupped his cheek before kissing him tenderly. She loved him so much.

Ethan gathered her close and held her, and everything was okay. Rose was safe. Arezo had hope for the future. Jade couldn't wait to be able to call the woman's family and let them know their daughter was still alive.

And she had Ethan. She held him close and listened to the sound of his steady heartbeat beneath her ear.

If you had told Jade a year ago that her life would change so drastically, she would have laughed. She'd been deadened by the past for so long. Now, the one holding her close was living proof it was possible to come back to life again.

She pulled away and looked into his eyes. "I love you, Ethan. So much."

He brushed back her hair and smiled. "I love you, too, and I can't wait to see where the future will lead us…together."

EPILOGUE

One year later...

He couldn't wait to get home. The rescue mission had ended in a happy result—he and his team had found the young climber who'd gone missing.

Ethan watched the lights of the ambulance disappear into the early morning. Mason stopped beside him.

While Ethan was grateful for God's help in finding the young woman, his thoughts were all for Jade. Today was his wedding day, and he couldn't wait to marry her.

Through everything they'd gone through in the mountains, God had made him realize his next chapter of life was to be spent with Jade.

"You looked bushed, my friend," Mason said with a grin. "We'd better get you home so you can rest before this afternoon, otherwise Jade will never forgive us."

Ethan smiled at the comment. They both knew differently. He'd told Jade about the missing climber as soon as the call came in, and she'd encouraged him to go because that was just who she was.

In the months following the rescue, Rose had fully recovered from the trauma, but Arezo's path to healing was much slower. Her memories of her family and growing up in Afghanistan had returned, but her doctor believed she'd blocked out everything about the abduction and what was done to her.

Her family had managed to escape the current situation in Afghanistan thanks to Jade and some of her friends at the FBI. Their arrival here in Montana had worked wonders for Arezo. Her doctor believed in time those memories could return, or she might never remember what happened. In Ethan's opinion, that might not be a bad thing.

Yoder had been sentenced, and they'd learned his motives for wanting to destroy the country stemmed from a thirst for power and control that drove him to do terrible things.

Fletcher finished speaking with the rest of the rescue team before joining them. "That was a close one. The paramedic seems to feel she will recover despite the frostbite." They started for the SUV.

"That's good to hear." Ethan climbed behind the wheel and left the mountainside as the first rays of sunlight filtered through the trees. They were close to Jade's cabin, and he couldn't resist the desire to talk to her, even though he wasn't supposed to see the bride before the wedding.

"I'll only be a second," he said when Mason tossed him a look. Neither commented on the *Englischer* tradition.

Ethan turned onto her road and drove the distance to the cabin. The lights were on. Jade had told him that since leaving the Marines, she hadn't been able to sleep late.

As soon as he stopped the SUV, the door opened, and his future stepped out to meet him.

Ethan's smile spread wide as he ignored both brothers' laughter.

She stood on the porch waiting for him to come to her.

"How was the rescue?" she asked without taking her eyes from his.

"A success. The young woman is on her way to the hospital, and the prognosis is good."

"Thank You, God." Jade hurried down the steps to hold him close. "I'm so glad I'm marrying you today."

He tipped her chin back and kissed her tenderly. "Nothing is going to stand in the way of me making you my wife."

She beamed at him, and he took in every inch of her pretty face. Since they'd survived Keller's attack, Jade had sought out professional help to process her abduction and rape. She was slowly learning to deal with what had happened to her in Afghanistan.

Keller and Yoder were facing treason charges and would no doubt be in prison for the rest of their lives. Those who were part of their devious plan were slowly being arrested around the world. A major attack had been prevented thanks to Jade's dogged pursuit of Keller.

"I should go," he said. "I know I shouldn't have come before the wedding, but I couldn't resist."

She touched his chin where the morning's stubble needed shaving. "You look tired, babe."

He enveloped her hand in his and kissed her knuckles. "Nothing that a few hours' sleep won't cure."

She glanced past his shoulder to where Mason and Fletcher were watching their exchange. "I'm so glad they both agreed to be part of the wedding."

Ethan looked to his friends, who quickly glanced away. "Yeah, me too. They're my best friends."

She smiled. Both Rose and Arezo were going to be Jade's attendants, and Walker had agreed to walk Jade down the aisle. The wedding was taking place at Ethan's ranch, and he prayed the weather would hold on as it had been for the past few days. Sunny and just a touch of crispness in the air.

He kissed her long and lingering before letting her go. "I'll see you in nine hours. I'll be easy to spot because I'll be the happiest man alive."

There were tears in her eyes. Jade had been crying a lot lately, mostly out of happiness, she claimed. "Nothing is going to stop me from marrying you, Ethan Connors. Absolutely nothing."

"Your ride is here. Are you ready?" Rose stuck her head into Jade's room. When she got a good look at her sister in her wedding dress, she exclaimed, "Oh…you look beautiful." Rose came into the room and closed the door. "I still can't believe my big sister is getting married."

"I can't either." Jade smiled at her reflection in the mirror. Her dark hair had been secured into a bun at the nape of her neck. She and Rose had found the perfect wedding dress in a tiny shop in Billings. It was simple and no frills—like Jade. The A-line chiffon dress had a square neckline and open back. Its floor-length skirt included a sweeping train. Jade had loved it from the second she'd tried it on.

With a final glance at herself, Jade looped her

arm through Rose's and stepped from the room. Arezo waited in the living room with her parents.

Jade was so happy they'd been able to get Arezo's parents out of Afghanistan after it had fallen to the Taliban. In the months since they'd found Arezo, she'd made remarkable progress, but it was having her parents with her that had fostered the most improvement.

Arezo rose slowly and straightened her dark blue chiffon lace dress.

"You both look beautiful," Jade told her sister and Arezo.

Someone knocked on the door, and Rose hurried to open it. Sheriff Walker Collins stepped inside and blew out a long whistle. "Second to my wife, you're just about the prettiest bride I've ever seen."

Jade giggled. She'd gotten to know Walker and his wife better, and they'd become like family.

"Are you ready to get married? I just talked to your groom, and he made me promise I'd get you to the house safely."

Jade smiled up at him. She wasn't sure who was the most worried—her or Ethan. "Then let's not keep him waiting."

"Yes, ma'am." Walker wrapped her hand around his arm and stepped out into a beautiful fall day in the mountains.

Walker assisted her and her flowing skirt into

the passenger seat while the rest of her party slipped into the back. The vehicle pulled away from the cabin, and they drove to Ethan's ranch.

She loved Ethan. Probably had for a while before she'd finally let go of the past and its pain and accepted his love.

"Right on time." Walker glanced her way and smiled as they stopped in front of her future home.

Jade pulled in a deep breath and opened the door. Once her party had gathered around her, they went inside.

Arezo's parents headed to their seats. Jade realized her hands were actually trembling.

Soon, the music started playing. Rose kissed her cheek and waited while Arezo hugged her. Both stepped outside and slowly made their way down the aisle.

"Last chance to change your mind?" Walker said from close by her side.

He was joking, of course. She could never change her mind. She loved Ethan too much.

"No, I'm looking forward to marrying my lieutenant."

Walker smiled his approval. "Then let's go."

Jade placed her hand on his arm once more. Together they stepped from the house. Her eyes slipped past the crowd of guests to the man who had changed her life.

Ethan had never looked more handsome than he did right now in his dark tux. She pulled in a breath when his eyes met hers, and the love he had for her never ceased to surprise her. All those years when she believed herself to be undeserving of love, she hadn't realized she just needed the right man to show her how important she was.

A smile spread across his lips as she walked down the aisle amid the smiling faces of their friends. Her aunt and uncle were there, as were many of their friends from the sheriff's department and the West Kootenai Amish community. A laugh bubbled up inside her when she spotted Molly, Nimshi and Trackr seated near Ethan wearing collars made of flowers around their necks.

Once she reached the front and stood beside Ethan, Walker kissed her cheek and joined his wife.

Jade gave each dog a hug. They'd become like family to her. She loved each of Ethan's dogs, but these three, well, they'd been through so much together.

Ethan took her hand and faced her as they listened to the minister of their church recite the marriage vows.

Jade recited her vows as did Ethan. The rest of the wedding ceremony went by in a blur. She was thankful one of their friends had agreed to film it because Jade was positive she wouldn't remember anything before the minister pronounced them husband and wife.

Ethan kissed her tenderly. She could feel him trembling as well.

Together, they walked down the aisle to cheering.

Ethan stepped inside the house and turned her to face him. He framed her cheeks with his hands, and the sincerity on his face had her full attention. "I want you to know how blessed I am that you are my wife. I love you, Jade. So much."

She tugged him close and put her arms around his neck. "I love you, too." She kissed him and finally could breathe again. This was what she'd been waiting for, through every meeting she and Ethan had sat in on concerning Keller, where Jade had to relive again the horror that she'd suffered at his hands. Ethan had been her rock. Having him there had helped Jade tell her story.

The door opened, and she and Ethan broke apart. Rose and Arezo came inside along with Mason and Fletcher.

The congratulations from their friends made the day even more special. Each one knew what the couple had gone through separately and were happy they'd found each other.

Once it was time for the wedding meal, Jade

reached for her husband's hand and stepped outside and into the fading sun.

The day had been simple but perfect, and she was ready to be alone with her husband.

"Are you happy?" he asked, placing his arm around her waist and drawing her close.

She leaned her head against his shoulder. "More than I could have ever imagined. Thank you for saving me."

He looked deep into her eyes and knew that she wasn't just talking about the rescue mission he and their Amish friends had embarked upon to find her and Rose. With Ethan's help, she'd saved herself from a world filled with anger and bitterness. And she believed she'd helped Ethan open his heart up to love again as well. Jade would be forever grateful.

* * * * *

If you enjoyed
Amish Country Ransom

Be sure to read
Amish Wilderness Survival

Available now from Love Inspired Suspense!

Dear Reader,

When you're in the middle of a storm, it's hard to see beyond the waves. We're caught up in simply surviving. If we count on ourselves for answers, we fail, but when we fix our eyes on God, He will guide us through even the worst of storms.

That's what happened to Jade Powell in *Amish Country Ransom*. Jade suffered a horrendous attack while serving in Afghanistan. She carried the pain and anger from that attack with her long after she left the military. Because of it, her life has been crippled by the past.

Yet when her sister is kidnapped by the same man who hurt her, Jade must find a way to move beyond her pain in order to save Rose before she suffers the same fate...or worse.

With the help of a man who knows a little about grief himself, her former lieutenant, Ethan Connors, Jade overcomes the nightmare she's lived with for so long and forges an unexpected bright future with Ethan.

So, no matter what storm you're facing, don't give up. Instead of looking to yourself for answers, look up. He's right there beside you waiting to carry you through.

Blessings,
Mary Alford

Get 3 FREE REWARDS!

We'll send you 2 FREE Books plus a FREE Mystery Gift.

FREE Value Over **$20**

Both the **Harlequin® Special Edition** and **Harlequin® Heartwarming™** series feature compelling novels filled with stories of love and strength where the bonds of friendship, family and community unite.